CabLab Publishing

cablabpublishing@verizon.net

First edition, 2011

First printing, 2011

ISBN #978-0615435206

ISBN #0615435203

DIP LITTLE

by

dav-wav rools

For Karla, an outlaw

Skateboarding was forbidden in Norway between 1978 and 1989 due to its supposed danger. The ban led skateboarders to construct ramps in the forest to avoid police.

1
Meet The *Nuevos*

" – gimme, dude!"

I snatch Rain's Zero even though he doesn't want to give it up. Who would? The Hawk tagged it at a Core Festival and Rain doesn't want it dinged. But he won't say no to *me*. We're best buds since k-class eight years ago. A lifetime.

I hop one foot on my own board and my other on Rain's Zero, and launch down Bicknell Hill riding on two skateboards.

"Yee-awww!" I shout, loud enough to scare old lady Baez down the block. We call her The PinchWalker since she walks like her shoes are too tight. She flinches and ejects her pet chihuahua ten feet high. Marcel lands on his paws though so it's OK.

Halfway down Bicknell Hill, I snag a crack and both boards fly out from under my feet. I skid to a stop on my butt and shred my expensive new board shorts on the concrete. I'm sure to hear about it from mom.

"Weak, lawyer son!" snickers Duane.

"Yeah? So when's the last time *you* did something rad?" I huff back. OK, maybe my pride's hurt.

Rain snickers too. "We oughta call you the Wipeout King, not the Skateboard King." But he grins at me when he says it. He knows not to count me out.

Every *Nuevo* on Santa Monica beach knows not to count out Dip Little. That's me. But that doesn't mean I don't get heckled like everyone else. I don't get any special treatment cuz I'm the boss of Bicknell Hill.

Duane chants: *Every Beach Has A Clown Who Thinks He Knows It All And He's Always Practicing His Cowabunga Call.* Rain and Trace stomp on the hot tar and some shrimp kid I don't know joins in. Someone says his name is Grody. *There's Nothing Worse Than A Gremmie Out Of Control.*

"You guys are such losers. Lemme see one of *you* double deck." I lick the blood leaking from my nose into my mouth. "I'll put up ten bucks for a pie if one of you makes it to the bottom."

My tenner buys a large Hawaiian pie at Perry's so everyone gives it a shot. One by one they crash without going further than me. Hah! One hour later, Rain and I are the only *Nuevos* still trying. I'm bruised and scraped but I won't quit, and neither will Rain. I guess he's as stupid as I am.

"Stop before you bust up," urges Duane. "You can't do it. I bet even the Hawk can't do it - "

- if there's something Duane can't do then he doesn't want anyone else doing it either. Whatever it is.

"Oh, yeah? Just watch."

Rain and I launch tag team down Bicknell Hill for the hundredth time. Me, I don't make it twenty feet before I ram the curb, wipe out and open gash #379 on my knee.

"Give it up, lawyer-son."

Behind me, Rain skims over the crack I wiped out on and completes a clean run to the bottom. He's beaten me this time.

The *Nuevos* bang their boards against the bus bench, knowing they'll double soon too. That's how it works. Once one of us gets it, the rest do too. Rain cuts a notch in his board for luck and we coast over to Perry's pizza shack on the boardwalk. A large pineapple pie vanishes in seconds and I mean *seconds*. Afterward, everyone's still hungry.

Rain eyes the blob of burnt cheese on my paper plate. "Gonna eat that or what?"

I shield the cheese just to bug him.

"I mean, if you're gonna eat it, fine, but if you're not - "

Rain'll eat pizza as black and crusty as King Tut's mummy if I give him the chance. So I push my plate beyond his reach. OK, so maybe I'm pissed he out-skated me.

Rain's not giving up on my cheese that easy. "See the smokin' blonde?" he says, pointing to a *numero uno* queen bee sashaying down the boardwalk. "It's *The Peach!*"

"Whoa, *The Peach*? Where?" Duane leaps up and flips over his scuffed plastic chair in the process. Stacy Peach has that effect on guys my age. In fact, she has that effect on guys, period.

"That's not her," says Duane dismissively.

"Says who - "

" - *she* doesn't come here. They say she doesn't like the beach - "

" - who says - "

" - to see Dip maybe she would - "

Yeah. No thanks. Don't remind me what a clown I've been about The Peach. Whenever I hang with her she plays me off against Kyle Gibson.

Rain hisses, " - she's looking at *you*, Dip!"

The possibility, however unlikely, suckers me into craning my head around. Immediately my unguarded cheese slides down Rain's throat. He got me again, and worse, the queen bee isn't even The Peach. That bums me out although I'd never admit it. I say I'm over her, but I'm not, no matter how bad she makes me feel.

I feel a tingle. My BlackBerry. Again. Ugh. Mom makes me carry the stupid thing like I'm a dog on a leash. Her constant checking on me is a reminder how far I am from being a *Viejo*. No old-school *Viejo* surfer has to check in with his mom. *Viejos* soar above meal times and curfews and buzzing BlackBerries.

GRMPA LST. PLS FND.

I make a face. Grandpa Little, aka Big Dip, is the one should be carrying the BlackBerry. But mom could never make him. She can't make him do *anything*. He may be eighty-something but he used to run the history department at Yale and he still runs his own show, at least around our house anyway. Forget trying to make him do what he doesn't want to do.

Did I say he reminds me of me?

"What's the bulletin, lawyer-son?" Duane never gets tired of ragging me that my parents are a couple of uptight lawyers.

"I got a new assignment. Big Dip's lost."

"Again? He got lost yesterday, didn't he - "

" - yeah. I tracked him to the Promenade."

"We heard. Everyone heard. You're the man for whacking Kyle Gibson."

See, yesterday Big Dip went to the movies by himself. Coming out he got mixed in with a bunch of John Adams poppies. The so-called popular kids at my middle school hate me and I hate them back. So no big surprise that the head poppy, my sworn enemy Kyle Gibson, played a stunt on Big Dip just cuz he's my grandpa. Kyle tricked Big Dip into telling the poppies a story about the good old days. Then Kyle circled behind grandpa and jumped up and down, making the cuckoo sign.

Lucky thing my mom had sent me on search and rescue. When I showed up, just one glance at my grandpa's confused expression filled in the picture.

I got right up in Kyle's face. "Gibson!" My cheeks were bright red under my freckles, like I was on fire.

"What of it, Tomato Face? Should I be scared?"

Kyle windmilled his fists in my face to show he wasn't taking sass from a chump skater. Even me. After all, his fat football body outweighs me by forty pounds. I'm five-ten but I only weigh one fifty.

In an instant, the poppies formed a circle around me like a pack of hyenas. But Kyle and his poppy posse didn't scare me. I was so angry I hissed like a tire with the air shooting out. Then I struck! I kicked in Kyle's knee so fast it even surprised me. He collapsed like a melting iceberg, the sneer still on his face.

"I'll get you, Little," he sputtered. "I'll crush you!"

Although slumping like a flat tire, Kyle kept up the bold talk. But he came off like a black angus mooing in a

11

slaughter-house. Even his poppy buddies smirked, like he was a hundred dollar-bill dropped in a dog turd.

"I'm waiting for you, football zit!" I yelled, and took my grandpa home. "Come and get me!"

That was yesterday. Ancient History. But I have to tell you about it so you know how it really is at our house. It's not perfect like people think.

See, this memory thing of Big Dip's has our whole family on edge. It's the eight hundred-pound gorilla no one names. Even my dad refused to acknowledge Big Dip's condition until Big Dip came to live with us while he mended from a broken leg. Big Dip had intended to return to the Big Dipper once he healed up, but his broken leg turned out to end his sailing days.

Nowadays, Big Dip sleeps in the spare bedroom downstairs and spends his afternoons on the porch watching me surf. Or listens to my sister Jesse fight with her boyfriends on the phone. He says Jesse and I are his own private reality show.

Dad never actually said it but I'm guessing Big Dip had to quit sailing cuz of how he gets ... *confused.* It's a problem that comes and goes. One day he's sharp and the next day he gets lost going to the store. M & D are a couple of professional problem solvers but this is one condition even they can't fix.

So what's everyone do? Send me on search and rescue, that's what. There's no second option. No one would dream of locking Big Dip up somewhere.

Duane peers at my BlackBerry screen over my shoulder. He's such a bug. "What's wrong with the old guy he can't get home by himself?"

I hate it when people make a big deal out of a little spacey behavior from my grandpa. It bothers me more than enough without being reminded. See, Big Dip and me have gotten tight over the last couple years. When I'm not getting along with M&D, he gets me talking and before I know it I'm spilling out things I never knew were inside me. So his memory's not so hot. We'll handle it, him and me.

Duane won't leave it alone.

"Dig this, lawyer-son. My cousin Ron's cocker-poodle, Munchy, jumped out of his pickup driving on Van Nuys Boulevard. The mutt totally disappeared. Then two days later Munchy showed up back home twenty miles away. Now if even a dumb dog can remember how to get home then you'd think your grandpa could remember - "

" - shut up!" snaps Rain.

He flicks Duane on the ear. Might not seem like a lot but it shuts down Duane's engine. Temporarily, anyway. Duane never shuts down for long.

"Gotta go," I mutter to the *Nuevos*, and bob my head like we Locals do to say goodbye. What would *you* say if your buddy had compared *your* grandpa to a cockapoo?

Did I mention how Kyle blabs at school that Little Dip (that's me) is bound to lose it like Big Dip? Kyle says the Flakeboard King (that's me) is halfway in the loony bin already.

As much as I hate Kyle, I'm secretly afraid the football-head may be right. See, Big Dip and I laugh at the same jokes and eat as much spaghetti as we can stuff in our mouths and hang at the beach no matter if it's sunny or rainy. Maybe Kyle's right that what's happening to Big Dip will happen to me too some day.

So? Go ahead and bring on your *some day*.
Everyone knows that *some days* are a long way away from now.

2
Big Dip

One by one the *Nuevos* bob their heads back and drift off in search of the next cool thing. Not Rain. No matter what goes down he sticks with me.

But where we gonna find Big Dip?

It's Sunday so I figure he's probably at Venice beach. Even if he's old, Big Dip gets a charge out of the whack scene there. Rain and I head that way on the boardwalk, Rain yakking about some ancient Bluetorch video of Kelly Slater surfing at Lower Trestles.

"Remember the backing track? Rad guitar."

I only grunt.

"Whaddya like better, Thrasher or Metal Edge? Catch the latest on Skatedork.com? Seen the new boards at Horizon West? Wish I could buy one."

Rain's chatter lifts me up after awhile.

"Ignore what Duane said. Your grandpa's cool. No matter what goes down he's still like us. Not like *them*!"

Rain points at the busker wannabes lining the Venice boardwalk, each with a gimmick for shaking loose spare change from the *turistas'* fanny packs. You ask me, the wannabes get way lost in the celebrity thing. Take our Shake Shack delivery guy, Rodney. A German *turista* told me he looked like John Mayer so now he spends every weekend strumming on a battered Stratocaster. His girlfriend is a Cher impersonator who pounds on a broken tambourine left over from the Summer of Love.

Ancient History.

We board-weave between the vendors selling cheapo t-shirts and sunglasses guaranteed to break in ten minutes and my sneaker *slap-pushes* mongo on the asphalt. We pass by a skinny dude who juggles two chain saws and four rubber chickens and reminds me of Michelle's dad in my algebra class. Come to think of it, he *is* Michelle's dad! And Ruffina the OWB (One Woman Band) who plays five instruments using her arms, legs and chin. Ruffina sure does a mean slide guitar with her big toe.

Vendors stretch on for blocks, selling everything from henna tattoos, three-minute massages and fortunetelling, to candles, cheap perfume, knock-off watches and incense sticks. Everything a *turista* might take back to China or Mexico or Germany before realizing the stuff was made there to begin with.

I don't see Big Dip, but there's an ugly hulky guy who shoots me a glare like he means to snap my head off. I glare right back.

"Dip, why's Kyle's older brother mad-dogging you?"

Uh-oh. So that's Kyle's brother Little Timmy? No wonder he's so ugly. And huge. He must be six-three and two-thirty.

"He's probably pissed I bashed in Kyle's knee yesterday."

"You *what*?" Rain pushes harder to put more distance between himself and Little Timmy. "Better change your name and move to Bakersfield. Better yet, make that Tokyo."

"Ha ha. Funny. Gotta find grandpa first."

"Ever consider that maybe he's not here?"

"He's *always* here on Sundays."

Rain nods at the mass of oily burning flesh around us. "Even if he is, we could hunt for hours and not find him."

"OK. You split. I won't leave without him."

I drop down on a bus bench, doing my best to avoid the melted popsicles and bird poop. The sunburned *turistas* pass by toting their umbrellas and plastic igloos to their SUVs and leaving only their trash behind. If they're gonna invade *my* beach why can't they at least take home their trash? I did mention that I hate *turistas*, didn't I?

At the waterline a white puff of hair ruffles atop what at first glance seems a broomstick. It's Big Dip wading in the shallows. With a tiny shock I realize how thin he's gotten.

"Hey, grandpa. It's go-home time."

I feel bad talking to him like he's five years old. But what choice do I have if he's confused? See, I'm never sure who I'll find when I go out on S & R. He can be either a wise old geezer or a silly old man. Lately, he's often just sad and tired. If M were around she could deal with Big Dip's sadness. But I don't know how. It's not something we dudes do.

"Mom's got lasagna for dinner. Bet I can eat the whole pan. How 'bout you?"

Usually, a mention of grub gets Big Dip on track, but not today. He frowns and digs his feet in the wet sand so it'll take a construction crane to pry him loose. He tugs on my arm and points at the ocean. Something special? Nah. Just some pelicans dive-bombing the chop and a dolphin bobbing about in the waves.

"Same old, same old."

Big Dip shakes his head and his white hair, almost as long as mine, blows in the breeze. "All stinkers and only *one* boat."

Stinker is Big Dip's name for the motorboats and SeaDoos that zigzag across Santa Monica Bay. Big Dip hates things with motors and considers sailboats the only boats worthy of the name.

"Yeah, I see a green sloop. Sorta looks like your old boat in the Bahamas. Is that what you mean?"

Big Dip's thin shoulders shake and right off I get it. He must feel like that fast-disappearing sailboat himself - alone and headed out of reach.

3
A New Job

Once I get Big Dip across Neilson Way and up the steps to our house, I'm off search and rescue duty. About time as I've got my own fish to grill. Like, is Little Timmy Gibson, Kyle's bro, out to get me? That's all I need. Not one but two fat Gibsons out to squash me like the week-old sandwich in my locker that I keep forgetting to throw out.

I sneak in the kitchen, hot on the trail of the aroma of lasagna, when I hear, "That you, Dip?"

Busted. It's grub I want, not a confab with my dad. See, he's a great guy like they say, but we're *so* different. We're both tall and thin but after that we go in different directions. Me, I'm on the boogie path, and dad he's on the serious path. My hair's long, stringy, and bleached colorless by the sun and saltwater. Dad s is dark and buzzed short. I rock. He listens to jazz on NPR.

You get the picture. I'm a dreamer and dad says that if you follow your dreams too much you'll wind up with nightmares. Yeah, well, my own idea of a nightmare is winding up as a lawyer, dad.

21

Still, I'll be the first to say that dad's a solid guy. He may be a chair-sitter but he's always there for me. Like Rain and Big Dip.

I poke my nose in the living room. M & D are sipping red wine with a chunky guy with an orange head of hair that's a cross between a Halloween pumpkin and a flattened traffic cone.

Mom runs her "never misses anything" eyes up and down me. "You shower yet?"

Ask me, she already knows I haven't. It's a game we play. I don't shower and she bugs me about it. I think it's her way of pretending I'm still six years old. Although she's seriously protective about her shiny maple floors too. Like, sand's gonna hurt 'em? Geez.

I go rinse off under the backyard shower. Used to be I'd snap my towel at Jesse and she'd scream and throw a dirt clod at me. But since she transformed into a poppy she's not around much anymore. How my annoying older sister became POPULAR is a genuine mystery.

Inside, I prowl the kitchen again for a snack. An open bottle of wine stands on the counter and a pot of red sauce bubbles on the stove. I test the sauce and then walk in the living room to see what's up with the oldsters.

Dad gives me his be-polite-or-you're-in-deep-doo-doo look. Did I mention that he actually says doo-doo?

"Dip, this is Superintendent Sandy Hanson from Zion National Park. He's my oldest buddy in the Park Service."

I shake hands and flash my five thousand-dollar post-orthodontia smile. "Pleased to meetcha, old buddy of Dad."

M&D smile approvingly.

"Just call me Super - "

" – Pumpkin?" I blurt before catching myself.

Dad winces but the Super laughs good-naturedly. Maybe it's not the first time he's been mistaken for a Super Pumpkin. "Super Sandy will do," he says lightly.

See, since my dad got out of law school he's worked for the National Park Service as a roaming troubleshooter. It's not legal stuff. More like problems that the NPS can't handle itself. They send him around the country and sometimes he takes me along. But Zion is new to me. I don't even know where it is.

"Zion's in Utah, Dip." It creeps me out when my dad reads my mind like that. "Super Sandy needs a detective there."

Okay. But what's this got to do with me?

Hmmm ... I wish it had something to do with me. Maybe I can worm my way into this. Spring break just started and I'm available.

"Strange doings," says the Super. "Check out these pits that showed up out of nowhere." He hands over a couple of eight by ten photos. "Would you believe it, your dad was a wild man twenty years ago."

No. I don't believe it.

Dad and I glance at photos of pits that look like graves, except they're too big to hold humans. "These babies gotta be ten feet deep," says my dad in surprise. "How many are there?"

"Hmph!" snorts the Super. "I'm still trying to find that out. I have no clue who dug them or why. But I won't stand for it. No one can vandalize *my* park right under *my* nose."

"What's there worth digging up?" I ask.

"My first guess is it's Anasazi Indian pottery," suggests my dad. "Native American artifacts are worth a fortune and professional pot hunters loot the Southwest for them. Some unscrupulous collectors don't ask any questions about where their pots came from."

Pots? Like my mom's saucepot hanging in the kitchen? Speaking of saucepots, when's that lasagna gonna be ready?

"Indian pottery was *my* first thought too," says the Super. "But the park historian says no Anasazi ever lived in Zion."

"Why don't the Ana-snozzy make more pots if people want 'em so bad?"

"It's Ana-sazi, Dip," corrects my know-it-all dad, "and they're long gone. The Ancient Ones disappeared before Columbus. Heard of that dude?"

"Yeah, dad. I know all about Chris Columbus." Like I'm supposed to know about the Ana-snozzy?

Super Sandy breaks in. "Rob, I need your help on this assignment - " he pauses - "but it may be too big a job for just one detective." His eyes flick toward me. "Got an extra one handy?"

"Might be too big a job for two detectives," I say. I have a third gumshoe in mind. "Spring break for me and Rain starts tomorrow!"

4
What's A Local?

Some things my mom can't get through her head no matter how many times I explain them.

"Okay, let's try it again. What's a Val?" she asks after breakfast the next day.

Outside, the surf's mushy and the beach boardwalk's quiet. My dad and the Super are chatting on the porch and Jesse's getting ready for a "romantic" picnic with Chopper. I suggested to Jesse that her boyfriends should all wear color-coded bracelets to tell them apart and she conked me in the head with an orange. I must be getting slow.

"Vals come from the San Fernando Valley, right?"

Mom's mixing snicker-doodle cookie dough and watching the news crawl on CNN. She never does one thing when she could be doing two or three. Like when she used to practice law she divided her day into Work Time, Personal Time and Home Time. HT had a funny way of being WT too. I should know. I was the Home Time.

That's when I began spending my spare time at the beach. There were the *Nuevos* to hang out with and the Pacific Ocean was always there, day or night, in good weather or bad. You couldn't always say the same for my mom.

After Big Dip came to live with us, M & D announced that they'd Done A Lot Of Thinking and reached some Serious Conclusions. Mom took a leave from work to spend quality time with Jesse and me. But Jesse was already at SAMOHI so it was too late for mom to smother *her* like mold on old bread. Instead, mom focuses on making up for lost time with me. That's how she is. She means to do the right thing.

But since middle school I'm not around much, and mom and I still haven't mastered that re-connecting thing. Like, she still can't tell the difference between a Local and a Val. Pathetic. I'm sure she learned a lot in law school, but no way she took a class on the subject of Vals.

It's not hard to get. A Local lives in Santa Monica. Younger Locals like me and Rain are *Nuevos,* and older Locals are *Viejos*. Everyone else we call a *Val* whether they live in the San Fernando Valley or not.

We Locals don't care for Vals. They have a lot of nerve breaking out of their cookie-cutter housing tracts and swarming over *our* beach like a cloud of flies hunting a dead fish. We can spot them a mile away by their too-shiny-got-it-on-my-birthday wetsuits and they're too dense to realize that the graffiti on the lifeguard towers is aimed at *them*.

Locals Only. Vals Go Home. Locals Rule.

That means you, dude.

"It's like this, mom. *Viejos* are Locals who've surfed here forever. *Nuevos* are the Locals my age - "

" - how can you be certain that you're a Local - "

" - if you are you know. Period."

Maybe mom is dense about this Val-Local business cuz she didn't grow up AWOL. Always West Of Lincoln. Lincoln is the dividing line that separates our beach neighborhood from Nowheresville, that is, all points inland. Then again, maybe mom plays dumb just to bug me.

No matter how dense she can be about Vals, my mom is a hundred times cooler than Rain's mom. At Back to School Night, Woman Bowman (changed from Louise Alice Bowman) tells anyone who doesn't flee fast enough that she's X-H (ex-hippie) and not so sure about the X part. She brays how the best day of her life was hanging out backstage with Country Joe and the Fish at Woodstock. Wasn't that 150 years ago? Talk about your Ancient History.

Woman is notorious in our 'hood for her mermaid costume fashioned from green plastic kelp. At first she only wore it to the annual Heal The Bay festival but now she wears it everywhere, even to the mall. She says she does it to draw attention to the environment although most people think it's to draw attention to herself. When she says, All the world's a stage, what she means is, All the world's HER stage. Which leads me to something else.

Rain Bowman. Rainbow Man. What's up with that?

Rain tells people that he's Native American on his dad's side and Rainbow Man is a tribal name. He says the reason his dad is never around is that he's off on a *vision quest*. It must be a never-ending quest cuz I know everyone Rain knows and I've never met his dad. A few people buy the Indian story cuz Rain's got straight black hair and eyes as black and shiny as obsidian. But the moms think that Rain's dad isn't a Native American on a vision quest, he's a scammer on the run from child support payments. Whatever. It doesn't change the fact that Rain's only contact with him is a few postcards now and then.

His parents may be flaky but Rain's as solid as they come. I guess he had to be. Someone at his house had to be a grown-up.

Mom spoons different-sized gobs of snicker-doodle dough on a greased cookie sheet. Betty Crocker she's not.

"What about me? Am I a ... *Vieja?* "

" - no offense but you're not anything, mom. You're just *old*."

Avoiding her towel snap, I snatch a fistful of cookie dough to nibble on and wander into the backyard. Big Dip is rinsing off under the outdoor shower.

"Ever wish you had a different name?" he says. He catches the droplets from the spigot in his mouth just like I do.

Big Dip sure comes out of nowhere sometimes.

"Why, grandpa? I wouldn't want to be a plain old Michael."

"*Dipfield* ... it's a name that belongs to an old man, not a boy your age."

Something's been on my mind. "Grandpa, why do you call me *Dipfield* instead of *Dip* like everyone else?"

"*Dip*'s a nickname. Only best friends use nicknames."

"Aren't *you* and *me* best friends?"

Before he can answer his eyes stare off in the distance and he slips off to Big Dip-land, just like that.

In the driveway, my dad is packing our Volvo for the trip to Zion. Packing is more than a chore to him, it's a complicated geometry problem. His eyes narrow as he compares the space in the car and the luggage at his feet, as if he's operating a 3D calculator in his head. I'd help but dad never goes along with my choices of placement.

Well, at least I didn't have to sweat him to bring Rain along. Dad can be a fun vacuum but I never have to tell him how much Rain misses his dad. Dad always brings Rain on board.

Did I mention that basically M&D are all right? I'll tell them. Someday.

Dad circles the Volvo for the best spot to stash our skateboards so they won't fly around in an accident. He spends a lot of time anticipating accidents.

"Dad, how come grandpa calls you *Robert* and not *Rob*. And he calls me *Dipfield* instead of *Dip*?"

Dad shrugs. "He's old-fashioned. He'll call you *Dip* when he's good and ready, and not a moment before."

5
Meet Banana-mouth

The thing is, going to Zion is good news *and* bad news. The good news is that I'm getting away from Kyle Gibson, his ugly brother Little Timmy, homework, stupid Mr. Warst in *Smart Teenagers Making Smart Choices*, The Peach and the snot-nosed poppies at John Adams Middle School. The bad news is, I'm leaving behind monster surf, Bicknell Hill, Perry's Pizza, the other *Nuevos* and Big Dip.

Still, a week of anything-can-happen sounds OK to me and if it keeps me out of trouble for five minutes it'll make M&D happy too. Although, hey, it's not *my* fault if I attract a bit of trouble now and then.

Like with Kyle Gibson. He's been picking fights with me since we were five years old. What am I supposed to do, lay down for him? I wouldn't take it from him when we were five years old and he outweighed me by ten pounds, and I'm not taking it today even though he outweighs me by forty.

And The Peach. When she pulls me in like an octopus extending its tentacles, what do M&D expect me to do? Ignore her? *Nobody* ignores her. Not girls, not guys, not teachers. She radiates enough babe-heat even Principal Tenzer stares at her in assembly. And for some reason lately she's focusing on *me*.

At a distance it seemed obvious how affected she is. But when she changed her seat to be next to mine in math, she got me too. Now I'm riding a rollercoaster that makes me sick but won't slow down long enough for me to get off. She can whisper to me when the teacher's back is turned and it's like no one else exists. Then a half hour later she's wearing Kyle Gibson's ratty Kobe Bryant jersey. Am I supposed to ignore *that*?

So OK, maybe I get in a bit of trouble. But M&D should realize that it's not like I go hunting for it. Trouble finds *me*.

Like two weeks ago in Mr. Warst's class, *Smart Teenagers Making Smart Choices*. I roll in a tiny minute late cuz I had to slag across campus from science lab and so what does Warst do? He stands me in the front like a salsa demo in a grocery store and fires trick questions at me. Like, what would I do if I found out my sister was pregnant? That's how Warst operates, he tries to nose around in personal stuff by pretending, what if? If you ask me, he's more like a peeper than a teacher.

No big surprise that Fern Randall butts in while I'm up front doing the salsa demo thing. She won't miss a chance to tell the entire class her personal business. Assuming that I'm off the hot seat, I sit down without being excused by Warst and next thing I know I'm in the VP's office for supposedly questioning authority. Huh? What authority? Mr. W has as much clout as a snow cone on a 95-degree day.

So yeah, escaping that band of crazies is A-OK to me.

Rain and I doze off while dad races through the Mojave Desert at his all-time high speed of 65 mph. Every so often I open my eyes and it's the same barren desert with a few mountains strung together in the distance. Who knows if there's a lizard the size of a dinosaur lurking out there? I wouldn't want to find out.

Dad exits the freeway at the Bun Boy in Baker, California, where the 30-foot high thermometer reads 112 degrees. We sprint across the parking lot like a sheet of molten black lava, and inside order double-burger baskets and french fry-onion ring combo platters. Yumm! It tastes even better to know what The Peach would say about it. "Ooh, this is soo unhealthy. Me, I never eat fried food. Never. Like, yuck!"

Not yuck. Yum!

Back in the car, Rain and I get trapped into listening to my dad work out the kinks in his pretend airline pilot routine.

"Welcome aboard, this is Captain Rob Little speaking. We've reached maximum cruising speed of 65 mph and we'll be passing through Las Vegas, Nevada at approximately 1400 hours."

"Pass through ... without stopping? Aw, c'mon, Mr. L – "

"Address me as Captain Little from now on. There will be no casinos, no sightseeing, and no Sin City For Children. It's pedal to the metal. May I have a volunteer cabin attendant come down the aisle and collect any trash - "

" - as if," I snicker, interrupting dad's, errr, Captain Little's spiel. That pilot routine of his wears out pretty quickly.

I pop in my earbuds and space out after that to sounds that Trace downloaded for me. He's famous for hunting down music that no one else even heard of. Not that I'd always know the difference. Like right now I'm listening to a Belgian group that reminds me of Ruffina, the OWB on the Venice boardwalk. Belgium ... Venice ... it sounds the same to me.

Slowly the desert transforms from California browns to Utah reds. Three hours later we arrive in Springdale, Utah, two miles outside Zion National Park. When dad slows down, Rain and I beat on the doors and chant, "We want out – hey – we want out –hey!"

Dad pulls over and Rain and I shove open the hatch and yank out our skateboards.

"We'll board to Zion lodge, dad."

"Do you know how to get there?" Dad eyeballs me narrowly. "FYI, Mr. Junior Detective, I say ixnay on the skateboarding in a national park."

"I say ixnay the ixnay, dad!"

Rain and I take off before dad can lay down any fresh rules for us to bust. We find a footpath that shortcuts the road to the lodge and it's our good luck that it's level enough to board on.

If I didn't tell you already, Zion is an awesome red rock canyon studded with cliffs rising hundreds of feet straight up. A slow-moving green river runs through the middle. Like Yosemite, if maybe you know that place.

Our path clings takes us by the river and under groves of cottonwood trees laden with light green leaves. Their white puffs float in the air all around. High above us, two tiny lumps, one blue and one yellow, cling like frightened bugs to the vertical cliff. We watch through the binocs as the colorful lumps labor up a pitch from handhold to handhold.

"Whoa, that's not the plastic wall in the shopping center food court they're climbing!"

"One slip and it's – splat."

"Maybe they'd only fall a little way since they're roped up - "

" - *if* the rope held - "

" - true, better not fall ... hey, how do they pee? Like, how's the one on top not hit the one below?"

Typical Rain. Wants to know how things work.

"If they peed when they're side-by-side - "

- in mid-sentence I snag a rock and sail clear off both my board and the path itself. When I get up I see ... *it*! A pit shielded by cedar trees like in the Super's photos.

I put my finger to my lips to shush Rain and we squat behind a mesquite bush to check things out. Just as we figure it's safe to come out, a shovel-sized clump of dirt flies out and lands at our feet.

I hiss in Rain's ear, "Someone's there!"

"No kidding, Sherlock. Either that or we just discovered the world's first dirt volcano."

Out of the pit pops a head on a long skinny neck like an ostrich. Whoever he is, he's got an oversize beak-nose that sniffs suspiciously in our direction. When he draws back his lips I see yellowed choppers set below eyes that bug out like a rodent on steroids.

Yuck! This dude is ugly. I mean, why doesn't he get a nose job like any sane person?

"This guy is a Banana Mouth!" blurts Rain in a muffled voice. "I got a question for him. Like, ever heard of toothpaste?"

"Rain, shush!"

Banana Mouth turns our direction, but seeing nothing hops back in the pit. Dirt flies out like he's a human steam shovel.

"Rain, let's nab him!"

"Are you nuts? You want to subdue him with your skateboard and arrest him?"

"Good idea."

"Get real. Fourteen year-olds can't make citizen's arrests."

If you ask me, Rain gets too caught up in the technicalities. I consider his point, then jump up and sprint for the pit before Rain can stop me.

6
The Stakeout

Halfway there I collide with an airborne dirt missile that smacks me in the kisser! Soon as I shake it off, the pit lurker clocks me with his shovel and knocks me on my butt. Funny part is, he hadn't seen me coming and KO-ed me by pure dumb luck!

After I come to, Rain tells me that once the Banana/Rodent Man realized he'd flattened me, he took off carrying a shovel and a metal detector. Rain knew it cuz geezers at the beach use them to hunt for jewelry lost in the sand.

I wobble to my feet and we board the rest of the way to the lodge, meeting Captain Little in the dining room.

"Holy cow, what train hit *you*?" dad exclaims. He's used to me getting shiners but he's pissed I got one *this* fast. We settle in at a corner table where a waiter fetches me an ice pack for my eye. "I want the whole story. Rain, you first." Dad shoots me his don't-worry-I'll-get-to-you-soon-enough look.

"It's like this, Mr. L. We're on our boards when Dip falls down, like usual. He fell next to a ginormous pit and we're checking it out - being careful like you'd want - when this ugly guy pops up. He's got the biggest beak-nose ever, not just skinny long, but BIG every which way."

" Ten-four," says dad. "Ugly. So what's up with Dip's eye?"

"Personally, I voted to stay put and not get involved. But you-know-who insisted on - "

I kick Rain under the table and give him my "that's enough" look, cuz dad may be old but he's not stupid. Especially when it comes to me. I know right away what's running through his mind. Just like me to jump now and think later.

OK, so maybe he's right.

I cut in before things go further downhill, skipping over the part where Rain tried to keep me out of it.

"This creep whacked me with his shovel - "

- dad groans. He and mom are always reminding me that I can't afford to lose any spare brain cells if I'm gonna get into Yale.

" - so here we are," finishes Rain.

Dad is busy digesting our story when Super Sandy shows up and orders three cheeseburgers and a French dip sandwich. Geez, he's a human garbage disposal. I'm sure not putting my hand in the way of *his* fork.

"More details on this yellow-toothed creep? "

" - tall and thin. Basically, a walking beak."

I'm waiting on a bison burger when I notice there's a mounted bison head glaring down at me from the wall. Whoever stuck it up there must have a sick sense of humor. Probably a vegan trying to freak out us burger-eaters.

Ha, ha. Won't work with me.

Rain kicks back in with Us versus Banana/Rodent Man.

"Beaky saw he whacked Dip, then squawked and took off."

Dad is thoughtful. "Squawked how?"

"In some mushy, oddball language."

"Hmm," grins my dad, "like Dip's English."

"He smelled smoky too. Tobacco-y but not regular smokes."

Super Sandy jumps in while waiting for his food.

"It's a start. We know more than we did a couple hours ago. I'll pass this on to my rangers and maybe we'll catch a break."

Seeing as no one has a plan for finding the Banana/Rodent Man, I make up my own. I mad-dog the bison head while I'm at it.

"Dad, my gut forecasts that the beaky guy will return to the scene of the crime. I say we stake out the pit."

I glance at Rain for backup but his eyes are on the waitress serving his pizza.

"Who's got the extra-large pineapple coming?"

"That's me," says Rain. "Set it here." He points to a place too far away for me to reach.

"And the burgers and French dip?"

The Super taps his place and the waitress sets down a Mt. Everest of food. Usually Rain is the biggest eater at any table, but the Super leaves him in the dust.

Rain chew-talks: "Where you gonna find a sucker dumb enough to stay up all night watching a stupid pit?"

" - you." I say, pointing at him. "You're the dummy."

"Who's *you*?"

"You're *you*! Who could be *you* except you?"

"Hold on," my dad breaks in. "No way you guys stake out this pit. Way too risky." He spears a chunk of bison steak.

"Thanks, Mr. L. Hear that, Dip?" Rain shakes his head. "You spell that R-I-S-K-Y."

Super Sandy is an eating-machine, he reminds me of a chipper that mulches tree limbs into sawdust. Rain glances at the Super's place enviously but there's no way he's getting his hand in the Super's way, either. "Let's hear Dip out," says the Super between bites.

"I'm talking good old-fashioned police work here."

"Dip, you're not the police."

"Yeah, so there," says Rain.

"So? This isn't dangerous. It'll be pitch dark and I've got my BlackBerry on me if we get in trouble."

"Pitch dark?" says Rain in a worried voice.

"Take it easy, Rain. That's the best part. The Rodent Man won't know we're there. I'll keep a low profile - "

" - you never keep a low - "

" - Rain has a point, Dip. Your track record's not so good – "

" - c'mon, dad, no worries. Relax and hand me a piece of Rain's pizza, wouldja -"

"- how do we see the Rodent Man without him seeing us?"

"He'll be too busy digging to see us. At least that's my plan."

Rain groans but I'm not concerned about convincing him. He won't get left behind. So maybe he dragged his feet when we boarded down Topanga Canyon Road. How was I supposed to know his front wheels would fall off?

My dad is the tougher sell.

"The rodent guy could be dangerous," he mulls. "All we know for sure is he swings a mean shovel and stinks like cheap tobacco. He could be an ex-con - "

Dad caves in when I lather on some soft soap about turning the stakeout into a hands-on learning experience. The education card always plays with M&D.

That night at 8:00 p.m., Rain and I set up in a hiding place with a view of the pit. We burrow into well-concealed sleeping bags and keep plenty of snacks handy.

I pop M&M's and dig on how ordinary sounds are mysterious in the dark. Rain sucks on a mango Snapple.

My dive watch reads midnight when I hear thudding footballs and see a light coming our way. It's him, or rather them. There are two voices grunting in the mushy language. I prop up on my elbows and focus the night vision binocs I borrowed from the Super.

Tall and thin as the Rodent Man is, his pal is the opposite. He's short and squat as a redwood stump. I cleverly decide to nickname him Chubby. They argue about something and the shorter one jabs the Rodent Man until the Rodent Man cuffs him back. They sound like two snakes hissing a duet.

"Call in your dad!" squeaks Rain.

"The action's barely started - "

" - if you don't, I will!"

Rain grabs for my BlackBerry and I push his hand away. Now I admit that I promised to call my dad at the first sign of trouble. But really, who considers this trouble?

"You promised not to do anything stupid."

"That was hours ago. We gotta catch these sneaks in the act before we bring in dad. They might be *turistas* - "

" - *turistas* at midnight? Are you nuts - "

" - OK, not *turistas*. *I* still have to catch them in the act – "

" - *you*? Why'd you bring *me* along if it's *you* who – "

" – I meant *us* - "

" - not *us* either. It's the Super should – "

" – geez, Rain, don't be a baby. If you keep Chubby busy I'll deal with the beaky guy."

Chubby has pissed off the Rodent Man cuz the latter barks a command and dirt really starts flying out. It rains down all the way on our hiding place ten yards away.

I decide I'm not waiting for an invitation so I rush over and ram the Rodent Man into Chubby. Chubby tips over but bounces back up like a boxing dummy. He seizes my arm and spins me around so fast that Rain's only a blur in the corner of my eye. When he lets go I sail into space like a stomp rocket. Then he grabs Rain and pitches *him* like a carny dishing out a stuffed animal. By the time we get to our feet, Chubby and the Rodent Man have scuttled off.

Rain flashes me his, You've-gone-and-done-it-again look.

Funny how well I know that look.

I limp over and dust him off. "Sorry, I screwed up."

He brightens. "Actually it was cool. It wouldn't be cool if we died but since there's no lasting damage - "

" - let's see what the sneaks left behind."

We max our flashlights and see a glimmer of half-exposed metal in the dirt. With my penknife, I scrape away the dirt until I free up an old-fashioned watch with an inscription on the back.

For Robert Parker from your grandfather. April 13, 1866.

"1866? That's not just Ancient History, that's prehistoric history," says Rain. "Who's the Parker guy? And why's anyone want his stupid watch?"

"Yeah." I nod. "Who cares about Robert Parker Nobody?"

7
Never Was A Cowboy

"No way the bad guys want a crummy watch."

Dad's too busy shaking his head to hear me. Ever since Rain and I straggled back to the lodge, Rain's been sucking down hot chocolate and I've been getting the third degree like I'm an outlaw. I try to focus dad on the bad guys but he keeps lecturing me on what I supposedly did wrong. All because I didn't sit on my duff and wait for some lawman with a tin star to ride to the rescue. When dad takes a break from complaining about out of control teens (me?) I mention the watch again.

The Super flips up an eyebrow. "Nice find. But probably doesn't mean a thing. Robert Parker Nobody is a red herring."

Rain looks up from a skateboard mag. "Red *hearing*?"

"Geez, red *herring*, dude." Sometimes Rain tunes in the wrong station. "You know, something to throw us off."

Dad's still sulky. "You didn't call like you promised."

"There wasn't time, it happened too fast." I take the offensive, never mind that it hasn't worked lately. "Give a little credit here, dad. Rain and I did the heavy lifting - "

" - *heavy lifting*?" smirks my dad. "It'll be a cold day in you-know-where when *you* do any heavy – "

" – that's a cheap shot, dad – "

" - before we jump to any conclusions, don't you think we should get the nitty-gritty on this Robert Parker Nobody?"

That's dad. Jump to conclusions? Never. Forget about jumping, period.

Super Sandy yawns. "I'm ready to sleep, not jump. These bad guys can wait 'til tomorrow to be caught."

"Hit the sack, Dip," orders my dad. "I don't want you so much as thinking about that pit. Can I trust you on that?"

Dad gives me the eye.

"Sure, dad. I'll stay out of trouble 'til morning ... *maybe*."

I grin to assure him I'm kidding. M&D can be slow that way.

Then I rap on Rain's noggin to rouse him from dozing and drooling on his skateboard mag.

"Time to scramble, Rain. Snooze at the cabin."

After that excitement, you'd figure we'd sleep until noon. But I'm wide-awake four hours later. Maybe the grayish light filtering in the cabin window wakes me. Anyway, I'm up and I want Rain up. I slam him with a pillow and tug him to his feet.

"Enough zzz's, Rain. It's time we go play."

"You can play for me. And do some leaving-me-alone while you're at it." Rain curls up and pulls the pillow over his head.

"C'mon, there's sightseeing on the menu. Super Sandy says no visitor to Zion should miss the Emerald Pools. If we leave now we'll catch the morning trail ride to them."

Rain's snoring so I fall back on the tried and true.

"The dining room has M&M pancakes."

Touche. In the lodge, I sneak our waiter a bag of
M&M's and tell him to sprinkle them on Rain's pancakes.
He shakes his head but does.

What's with this head-shaking thing people do to
me? M&D. Mr. Warst. Kyle Gibson. Now some waiter I
don't know and don't want to know. What's the big deal?
I don't get it. I mean, if I don't push nothing ever happens.
Nothing fun, anyway.

Like the time Kyle bragged in homeroom how he
finished third out of two hundred in the Punt, Pass and Kick
contest and would've won if his arm wasn't dead tired from
pitching a no-hitter the day before. Like that wasn't
enough, Kyle put on a sly look and sneered, Why don't *you*
play football, Dipstick?

Truth is, M&D won't let me. But I'm not gonna cop
to that, so I said, I got my reasons.

Kyle guffawed and flapped his arms like a chicken.
"Yeah, your reasons are named Cluck, Cluck and More
Cluck. You oughta change your name from Dip Little to
… *Chicken Little!*"

Huh? I backhanded Kyle in the chest and before he
could hit back Mr. W ambled in from the hall.

"Mr. Dip Little! Cease that violence immediately!"

Kyle gave me the I'll-deal-with-you-later and he and Warst did their headshaking thing in unison. Just the memory ticks me off. I don't care what you do, just don't shake your head at me.

Rain liked the M&M pancakes so much he tells our waiter he wants them again tomorrow with peanut M&M's. Stoked up on carbs, we hightail it to the stables for our Emerald Pools trail ride.

"Who's the boss of this outfit?"

A seriously crusted-over dude perched on the gatepost lifts his head at my question. He's dressed in a checkered western shirt, scuffed boots, chaps and a Stetson so dented it might have been stomped by the bison in the dining room.

"Name is Ten Bears."

"Huh?" Sounded like Ten Beards.

"Who're you? Not them scoot-boarders I hear about - "

" - that's *skateboarders*," replies Rain. "S-k-a-t-e- "

" - yep, I knew it. *Scoot-boarders*. Ready to trade them scoots for God's gift to man, the horse?" He points to two animals as big as houses. "Now these beasts are remarkable. On a good day they'll throw a rider fifty, sixty feet. Up fer that?"

"Uh … I guess so …."

"We are?" squeaks Rain. His eyes are the size of golf balls.

Ten Bears hops off the gate to inspect us and frowns. "Maybe you scoots should stick to mules."

"Horses scare me," admits Rain. "I got thrown once."

"Oncet? Never was a cowboy ain't never been thrown." He turns to me, "How 'bout you, pard? You been thrown?"

"No way," I say, trying to sound confident. He stares me down until I admit, "Actually, I've never ridden a horse."

Ten Bears sniffs. "Waaaaaul," he says, dragging out the syllable as if it's a piece of toffee. "Let's see if'n we can't change that." He calls out to a wrangler prepping a cinch. "Saddle up Thunderbolt for this here scootboarder."

The sun has crawled over the cliffs and glows eerily on the canyon walls. Do I need to say that the prospect of getting tossed by a house-sized beast scares me to death?

"Look, Ten Beards, I'm more of a surfer "

"Waaaul, ain't no waves here, mister scootboarder." He yawns and stifles a smile. "Fetch Thunderbolt."

When the wrangler leads over Thunderbolt, I get the joke. Thunderbolt is the saddest-looking pony in the state of Utah. He should ride me instead of the other way around.

Ten Bears chortles and spits a stream of chew. "Heh, heh. Got you there, scooter-boy!"

As if that's not enough, Thunderbolt nails me with a gob of horse spit.

"Yuck!"

Rain laughs so hard that he doesn't notice his own horse has shot a river of pee on his Vans and dyed them yellow.

Ten Beards's wrangler turns out to be a she, not a he. A she with an oval face, brown eyes and white blond hair stuffed under her Stetson. A country-style Stacy Peach.

"This here's Gopher," says Ten Bears when he sees me staring. "Heckit. No reason not to be riding."

Right off the she-wrangler takes charge. "Get this straight, you two, the name's Snow not Gopher. Like the weather. Besides that, you do what I say and maybe you'll come back alive." I must still be staring cuz she snaps her fingers. "Got that?"

"Got it," I say sheepishly. It's hard not to stare. Her eyes are as warm as the red-brown sandstone.

"Watch me mount." She swings weightlessly through the air and settles in the saddle. "Now you try."

Rain swings up in his saddle just fine. Not me. I go too far and end up sailing over my saddle and landing in the horse pee. Bet you didn't know how much horse pee stinks.

Ten Bears grins like he's drawn out on a fat poker hand. "Heh, heh. May be your first time being thrown, sonny, but sure as heckit won't be your last."

OK, so what if I'm a bit clumsy? I'm fast.

It's just Rain and me following behind Snow through patches of manzanita and sage. Our horses know the trail like I know the beach back home and they amble along, kicking up dust in the dry, sweet air. It's so peaceful it wouldn't surprise me to hear Rain snore. I know from personal experience that he'll sleep anywhere cuz I've seen him sleep with his head in a pizza box.

"Know what cowboys put on chapped lips?" asks Snow. "Horse poop. Won't heal 'em but it'll sure keep you from lickin' 'em."

I laugh half-heartedly.

"Lemme tell you about the time I found a mountain lion munching on a mule deer carcass."

Whoa. That perks me up.

"Yeah, you should've seem me smack the mountain lion in the mouth and say, I'm the one ordered the venison!"

Geez, talk about corny ... am I on a tour bus for seniors?

Snow sees my face and apologizes. "Sorry about that. Ten Bears makes me memorize a script with jokes for the *turistas*."

I redden. "OK, but you don't think me and Rain are *turistas*?" I gulp. "Do you?"

"No, no way," she says hastily.

After that, we jounce along and drift into the usual stuff about what grade you in, what school you at. When

Snow calls time-out we tie our horses in the shade and dunk our feet in an ice-cold creek. Snow cuts wedges of chocolate. Like usual, Rain grabs his *and* mine.

"How'd you get the name, Snow?"

She has a big, friendly smile. "My mom grew up back east and never got used to so much sunshine. She named me *Snow* to remind her of home. People say she had a great sense of humor." Snow's face falls. "She died years ago."

My face falls too. I can't imagine my own mom dead. Not Rain's mom either, although I wouldn't miss her *I Was Born At Woodstock* t-shirt.

"How old were you when - "

" - three. It's Ancient History."

"You're not the only one has a weird name."

"Yeah. What's up with *Dip* ... and *Rain*?"

I shrug. "Is your dad a cowboy?"

"Naah. He's afraid of horses. He's a prof at Utah State."

"What's he teach, some wuss subject like accounting?"

"Cowboy History. Dad's not a cowboy himself but he reads tons of books about them. He researches Old West mysteries and I help him."

She tosses me a pizza slice-sized wedge of chocolate and I jam it in my mouth before Rain can snatch it.

"Old West mysteries, huh? Ya don't say."

8

The Mysterious Watch

After that, we get along peachy (or maybe I should say, un-Peachy) and Rain awards Snow the highest compliment possible.

"Whoa, she'd be wicked on a surfboard," he says, as return on the road to the cabin.

"Yeah. Tough *and* pretty."

A car pulls up alongside. It's dad. Did I tell you how I go back and forth about him? Everyone knows he's a great guy and so do I. But he can be a fun vacuum. He wants me to be quiet and polite like him.

No such luck, dad!

Rain and I hop in and utter the magic word. "Food, please." Actually, that's two words.

"You got it, guys."

At the lodge we park amidst more tour buses spitting out *turistas*. No way anyone would mix us up with *them* ... is there?

"What'd you do while we went to the Emerald Pools, dad?"

"I drove to the history museum in Cedar City and came up with info that'd knock your socks off ... if you ever wore any."

The hostess seats us at our regular table and right away the stuffed bison gives me the evil eye. I order the double bison burger just to show him who's boss.

Dad brandishes his spoon like a symphony conductor to get my attention. "I confirmed a hunch I had that the real name of this Robert Parker Nobody is - "

" - yeah, dad?"

He pauses dramatically and waves his spoon like he's bringing in the cellos.

"C'mon, dad, fill us in."

" – Butch Cassidy!"

"Huh?" I don't have a clue.

"Robert Parker is Butch Cassidy? Far out."

It's the Super. He flops down and signals the waitress to bring his "usual." I'm beginning to think this guy lives in the dining room.

"Robert Parker aka Butch Cassidy was an old-time Wild West outlaw. His gang was called The Wild Bunch."

"Yeah? So what's his watch doing here?"

The Super licks his lips, visualizing the grub he's ordered. "Butch grew up here. His family came west in the 1860's as part of the Mormon hand cart migration."

"Handcarts? Mormon migration?" I'm lost.

"Pioneer Mormons got driven out of their homes back East and migrated to Utah," says Rain authoritatively. "They didn't have money for horses and wagons so they pushed the whole way in hand carts."

Leave it to Rain to know the Ancient History.

"OK, but how'd this Parker guy become an outlaw? And why's anyone want his watch?"

Rain jumps in. "Maybe the bad guys want something else. If we knew more about Butch - "

That gets my dad off and running.

"I read up on Butch at the library so listen up.

"To understand him you have to accept that he was both an outlaw *and* a good guy. He was the Robin Hood of the Old West. He he saved a priest in a snowstorm and another time he returned a stolen horse to a little boy."

"Outlaw Boy Scout, huh? Nice combo."

"Yeah," says my dad, stationing the salt and pepper shakers like cannons to protect his plate. "In 1899, Butch pulled off the biggest train robbery of all time. He robbed the Union Pacific's Overland Flyer. After that, Johnny Law got serious about tracking down Butch. The Wild Bunch got caught except for you-know-who -"

" - good old Butch," I put in helpfully.

"Yep. Butch and his sidekick - "

" - The Sundance Kid," finishes Rain.

"Very good," says my dad, pleased. "Didja see the movie?"

 Rain nods.

"Hey!" I yelp. "When'd you see a movie without *me*?"

"Butch and Sundance outran the law," says Rain smugly.

"Outran to where? An outlaw retirement community in Vegas?"

Dad points his spoon at Rain like he's calling for a big finish from the horns. He's got that dramatic flair thing going today.

On cue, Rain says, "That's what nobody knows."

9
The Wild Bunch

Anyway, dad thinks that Butch's old watch is our key to the pit diggers. If we get the scoop on Butch Cassidy memorabilia it may lead us to the next clue. So on the phone he sets up a confab for the next day with the biggest western collectibles dealers in Denver. Then he buys a plane ticket online while I try out my latest bright idea on Rain.

"Got your i-phone?"

"Right away, boss-man. I log on at your command."

"Gimme here and see how a real expert does it."

Rain rolls his eyes but grudgingly hands over his i-phone.

"While my dad spins his wheels in Denver, you and me'll move this case forward and not leave the snack stand, either."

I love the idea of beating my dad at his own game. For him this Zion mystery is just a job but to me it's a contest. A chance to prove I'm not the goof he thinks I am.

I piggyback on the lodge wireless service and punch "Butch Cassidy" in the search engine. Thousands of links pop up to Butch Cassidy poker chips, beer mugs, beach towels, baseball caps, t-shirts, newspaper articles, movies, books and even a dating service advertising dates with honest-to-goodness Butch Cassidy look-alikes.

"Junk, junk, junk," I mutter disgustedly. But I'm not giving so easy and I keep scrolling until I reach an archived article about the only photo taken of The Wild Bunch. The headline says:

What a steal!
Original Wild Bunch photo
nabs $135,000.

I scan forward.

This portrait shows
five famous outlaws: Butch
Cassidy, The Sundance Kid,
Elzy Lay, the Tall Texan and
Kid Curry.

After robbing a bank
in Nevada, The Wild Bunch
had their picture taken
decked out in derby hats.
Out of spite they sent it to the
president of the bank they'd
just robbed.

That turned out to be
their big mistake. Pinkerton
detectives posted copies of
the photo all across the
country.

Once their faces were
known, The Wild Bunch lost
the element of surprise that
made possible their
robberies. Butch and
Sundance had to run away to
South America.

"What a bozo!" laughs Rain. "Butch should've kept
it on the down low and not stuck his nose in trouble."

Hmm. Mom says the same thing about *me*.

A smoky smell sucks up my nose. Huh. Why, it's ... Rodent Man! I swivel and spot him - or someone just as ugly - lurking in the shadows. I punch Rain in the shoulder.

"Ouch! Cut it out, wouldja."

Wouldja back at ya - look!"

The pit diggers are twenty feet away, mingling with a herd of dazed-looking *turistas*. Rodent Man wears a black and silver Raiders sweatshirt and Chubby has on a Dodger jacket. Must be their idea of native camouflage.

"I smelled them before I saw them!"

"Yeah. And their beaky noses are a dead giveaway." Rain's forehead wrinkles. "Think they're following us?"

"Only one way to find out."

I rush forward with Rain trailing me for backup. But they see us coming and duck behind a tour bus. Before Rain and I circle it they're gone, leaving only their odor behind.

"Have smell will travel," sniffs Rain.

A woman wearing a Yellowstone N.P. baseball cap mutters, "Gaulloise. French cigarettes." She coughs. "Dreadful."

"It's a clue," I say hopefully. "Who smokes French cigarettes?"

"Duh ... French people?"

"But that wasn't French. Even *I* know that."

We head back to our cabin to find a sloppy handwritten note on our door.

GO HOME OR U BE SORRY.

Even the paper stinks.

10
Gopher For A Day

The next morning dad heads off to Denver bright and early. With my own personal fun vacuum out of the way Rain and I are free to explore Zion without interference. I touch base with dad mid-morning but my call goes straight to voicemail. I figure he's still on the plane until I get a text from him.

STAY OUT OF TROUBLE.

Yeah, right, dad. I'd consider it but trouble equals fun and no trouble equals no fun. Dad wouldn't see it my way. He and I never agree what's fun. We're from different planets. He's from the work planet and I'm from the fun planet.

Even without dad giving orders, I'm moving this case ahead. Dad's not the only one who can pick the brain of a Wild West expert. I peg Snow's dad, Prof Cone, for somebody with insider scoop on Butch Cassidy, but how do

I find him? I have the keys to dad's car but I don't have a learner's permit much less a driver's license.

Hey, it's not like I've *never* driven. Big Dip and I snuck dad's car over to the beach lot when dad was out of town and I drove in circles around the empty lot while Big Dip urged me to go faster.

Hmm.

I don't want to involve Rain in this scheme, so to throw him off I say, "Guess I'll go to the stables and see what's up."

"What's up?" demands Rain, sensing I've got something up my sleeve. "You're not meeting Snow, are you?"

"Well, not exactly - "

" - not so fast, hotshot. You're not Snow-seeing without me."

Having failed to lose Rain, we tramp to the stables where Ten Bears is perched on the same gatepost we left him on.

"Do you ever move, dude?"

Ten Bears shifts slightly.

"Expecting Snow?"

"Beats my two pair," grunts Ten Bears. "Not my beeswax when it ain't her day to gopher. Sure wish she was here cuz I'm right short-handed." He sizes up Rain and brightens, licking his lips like he's picking out a roast for supper.

"You!" he cackles and points at Rain. "Scooterboy!"

"*Me*? My name's Rain - "

" - ready to gopher?"

This could be my break. If Ten Bears keeps Rain busy I can get in trouble by myself. Rain hesitates, uncertain what gopher-ing involves. Frankly, so am I.

"He'll gopher no charge," I volunteer. "Rain and I are happy to help a friend in need."

"Gopher?" Rain glares. "Speak for yourself why don't - "

" - it's great," says Ten Bears, "to find a sucker, err, I mean, helper. So see them saddles on the rail? Go fer 'em!"

While Rain stands shocked, I hightail it to dad's car and dig out the key box under the wheel well. Just like that, I'm off.

So aside from the beach lot my only driving time is a go-kart at Duane's twelfth birthday party. What's the big deal? Go-karts have tires, pedals and a steering wheel too. What's the big diff?

11

The World's Leading Expert

I carefully ease dad's Volvo into the parking lot of the Bumbleberry Cafe in Springdale. So far so good. Maybe I bumped a couple of road signs on the way. Nothing that can't be repaired. I order a slice of bumbleberry pie from an old lady closing in on forty and she brings it with a big glass of milk. I ask if she knows the Cone family and she nods.

"Sure do, honey. I've known Snow since she was a baby and the prof since we were in kindergarten together. He was a geeky little thing. His nose was too small to hold up his glasses and he wore a rubber band to keep them up. Hasn't changed much."

"Which way to the Cone ranch?"

She gives me a sly look and punches me in the arm. "That Snow's a cutie, huh?"

I redden. "Yeah ... so, uhn, can you tell me - "

" - see the bridge? Cross it, two miles and take a right. Five miles and you'll see a house with green shingles and blue doors."

"This pie's the best and so are you!"

She laughs me off and I go to the car, proud to have made it through town safe and sound and be closing in on an interview with a Butch Cassidy expert. I cross the bridge and jounce along to a ranch house with green shingles and blue doors. It's the spitting image of my house in Santa Monica, except instead of being in the middle of *turistas*, cars, bikes, and strollers, the Cone house is by itself in the middle of nowhere.

The eerie silence is starting to spook me when a dark-haired man hulloes from the porch.

"What brings you out here, young fellow?" He gives me the once-over. "Sure you're old enough to drive?"

"Hi Prof Cone, I'm a friend of your daughter. She's bragged so much about you that - "

" - bragged about *me*?" He's pleased ... and surprised.

"Aren't you the world's leading expert on Butch Cassidy?"

"Hmm ... well ... I've often thought so."

Bingo, this guy is a pushover. "If you know more than almost anyone - "

" - *almost anyone*? My pinky finger knows more about Butch Cassidy than anyone else. What's your interest, Mr. Little?"

I decide not to open that door yet. Dad would be seriously pissed if I told the wrong person what we're up to.

"Uh ...." I search for a plausible fib. "I'm doing a report on Butch at school." I hold my breath to see if he buys it. Incredibly, he does.

"Excellent choice. The world doesn't know enough about Butch Cassidy." He pauses. "No matter how often I tell them." He pauses again. "Nobody listens to me."

It's easy to keep him talking after that, he's a Butch Cassidy fanatic. I'm not sure what I hope to find out but I figure I'll know it when I hear it.

" - Butch was a Local here, right?"

"Yep. Like me." The prof throws back his shoulders and puffs up his chest. "Born in the Midwest and came here as a boy. Ran away from home after almost killing a man. Turned his talents to robbing banks and carved out a place in American history."

Yeah, I think to myself. As an outlaw. "So you admire him?"

"Absolutely. He was clever." Cone pauses. "Like yours - "

- don't say it, I mouth silently -

" - truly." He clears his throat dramatically.

" - is it true that Butch ran off to South America?"

"Yes."

"And died there like history books say?"

"No."

"No?"

"No."

"So where'd he go?"

"Here! The great Butch Cassidy wound up at home," whispers the prof, as if telling me a secret.

"So why do the historians write he died in South America?"

"All historians but me are ignoramuses. I, I have evidence!"

"What's your evidence - "

" - ENOUGH, profezzur!"

The smell hits me first. I spin around and come eye-to-eye (well, make that eye-to-beak) with the Rodent

Man and his sunburned peeling beak-nose. Where he comes from they never heard of sunscreen.

"Dude, how come you smell like that?" I blurt, backpedaling to escape the unpleasant odor.

Rodent Man curls his lips like my neighbor's golden retriever at his snack dish. "Deep Leetle, yes? Zu are trouble."

I'm trouble ... how's he know? Has he been talking to M&D? And how's he know my name?

"Romo, don't be rude to Mr. Little," says the prof in a wimpy tone. "He's a friend of my daughter."

Hmm. Why's the prof cozy with the Rodent Man aka Romo? The prof doesn't seem like the type to get his fingernails dirty -

- then I get it. The prof's not digging, he doesn't even realize it's going on. The world's leading Butch Cassidy expert doesn't realize what's happening under his own nose.

"Why you come here, Meester Deep? For ze Snow Cone?" Romo leers. "Well, she's not here. So run along, leetle boy."

This guy's got nerve. I'm tempted to give him the Kyle Gibson knee treatment. No ugly stinker with bad teeth tells *me* to scat. But I hold off, unwilling to give away that I'm on to him.

"OK," I say, when who should run up behind me, all out of breath, but Snow herself.

"Hey you ... Dip!"

"Hey yourself ... Snow!"

We laugh nervously.

"Why are *you* here?" She's mystified. She takes me *turista*-ing and next thing she knows I'm camped on her doorstep.

"I came to see your dad about Butch Cassidy. I'm doing a report on him for school - "

" - yeah, and I'm Wonder Woman." She's not buying I'm a hard charger doing my schoolwork on vacation.

I suck in a breath and decide to trust her with the truth. "This is the scoop, but you can't tell anyone, not even your dad."

"What's up?"

"Romo and his fat sidekick are what's up - "

" - you mean his brother, Fumi?"

"Yeah. They're scheming to dig up something in the park. The Super brought me in to find out what."

"I know what it's about." She sighs.

"You do?" It's the last thing I expect to hear.

"They're digging for Butch's jewelry that my dad's spent years looking for. Dad's a fool to trust Romo."

"Butch stole jewelry? I thought he only robbed banks."

"This whole thing started with a trunk my dad bought from old lady Harris. See, my dad chases around to flea markets and garage sales for overlooked Old West stuff.

"Anyway, dad uncovered a letter that proves Butch returned to Zion from South America. If real it's a major Wild West find!"

"So why keep it secret?"

"Dad wants to be a hundred percent sure Butch actually wrote it before he goes public. He's screwed up before and he's gotten a reputation as a goof. This time around he has to be 100% right or he's finished as a scholar."

"Where do Romo and Fumi come in?" I think I know but I want to hear it from her. Before she answers, Fumi the human Sit 'n Bounce rolls down the hill, rams me and crams me in the Volvo.

"Go home, leetle Deep!"

I don't have a choice. Fumi slams the door before I can get O2 back in my lungs. I fire up the Volvo and head for the lodge.

12
One Angry BlackBerry

So much for my bright idea to pick the prof's brain. I would've gotten more info by picking my nose. The only juicy info came from Snow and not her dad.

Anyway, next morning I wake up to an obnoxious buzzing sound and assume it's Rain, snoring as usual. I grab a hiking boot to toss at him but it's not Rain, it's my BlackBerry, bouncing around on the nightstand and vibrating like an angry rattler.

"Yeah? I mean, hello?"

"Snow here. Wake up much?"

I perk up. "Hey you."

"I've got something to show you but I have to gopher for Ten Bears 'til lunch. See you after?"

"Sure. Let's meet at the stables at one."

I click off and poke Rain, who doesn't budge even when I tickle his stomach. I wonder what Snow wants to show me. Butch's letter? I'm not waiting to find out.

My BlackBerry vibrates with a text. No name. Blocked number.

DP. NEED C U.

Huh? That could be anyone from Mr. W to Kyle
Gibson to the girl with stringy black hair who stares at me
in bio. Or even Jesse's boyfriend Chopper. Or maybe it's
Sid. Whatever his name is, he's a jerk and I'm not sorry I
put glue in his bike chain.

"Geez, Dip. Why ya kicking me?"

"Get a move on, RainMan. We've a breakfast to eat
and a mystery to solve."

I yank Rain to his feet and drag him still stumbling
to the dining room.

"Whoa, I've had it with sitting by that buffalo," he
grouses. "It doesn't like me and vice versa."

"Actually, it's a bison, not a buffalo. But it's fine
with me if we sit by the moose. He's friendly enough."

Actually, when we get up close the moose isn't
friendly either. He's pissed and sad. I guess I'd be pissed
too if somebody stuck *my* head on a dining room wall.
Who dreamed up that idea?

When the waitress brings my bacon I'm glad there aren't any pigs in the vicinity.

"Pay attention, wouldja, Rain. I got us a lead ... err, Snow got us a lead - "

- my BlackBerry interrupts us.

"What's it say, dude?" mumbles Rain through a mouthful of pancakes topped with peanut M&M's.

DP. NED U.

"Who's it from?"

"Blocked number."

"Weird."

"Forget it. Let's get back to the mystery - "

"Let's not get back to the mystery," says Rain. "Let's skateboard. We can mystery-ize later."

Maybe it's time Rain got his way once. After he finishes his fourth plate of pancakes we hop on and board to Weeping Rock. It's a rocky cliff riddled with seeps oozing groundwater. Yellow columbine, red shooting stars and purple monkey flowers cluster at its seeps and glow like Christmas tree bulbs.

All fine so far, but something's bothering me, something that's been bothering me since we got to Zion even if I didn't know it right away. After four days away from home, it's not my mom, the beach, or Perry's Pizza that I miss like I miss ... *Big Dip*.

"He can be such a pain in the ass," I say out loud.

"Kyle Gibson?"

"No, my grandpa."

"Huh? He's cool, dude. You can't blame him for the goofy stuff he does. He's ... *old*."

"It's like his brain is frying and it scares me. It scares *me* more than it scares *him*. See, Duane told me how it went down when *his* grandma's brain fried. She got so bad she'd pick up her fork and forget she was holding it before she could take a bite."

"Duane's a pain in the butt. Big Dip won't end up like that."

"Hope not."

But I'm secretly afraid he will. I don't like imagining my grandpa forgetting how to eat spaghetti and meatballs. But what can I do about it?

I scoop up the stones where I'm sitting and pelt the helpless flowers that sprout from Weeping Rock. I do a guillotine job on a scarlet shooting star and chop its head clean off.

"When I was small, Big Dip visited us in the spring. After dinner he carried me to the beach. We sat on the sand, him and me, and waited for the stars to come out. He told me stories about the Caribbean ports where the wind smelled like orange juice and salt. He promised to take me there when I grew up."

I kick a rock and it skitters over the bank and makes a sound like a pistol shot.

"You're lucky you had him," says Rain. "My mom's parents don't visit and I never met my dad's folks."

"I'm not lucky. Not if you ask me," I mutter. "When Big Dip's gone who's gonna take his place?" I hold my breath so Rain won't see I'm crying. The funny thing is, it's not like I'm crying for my grandpa. I'm crying for me. Seems like when I reach out to hold someone they drift away. Mom. Stacy Peach. Now Big Dip.

He promised to take me sailing when I grew up, but now that I'm old enough he's *too* old. He's not a captain.

He's just an old man who can't get home by himself. What if he keeps going downhill and winds up messing himself and forgetting my name?

A cloud passes over the sun and the flowers aren't so pretty. I have a dark thought that I can't tell anyone, not even Rain.

If that's how it's gonna end up, what good is Big Dip anyway?

13
Wishing Rock

Next stop after Weeping Rock is the corral. I'm hoping to see Snow but we have to settle for Ten Bears, still perched on his favorite gatepost. Just the sight of the crusty old dude makes Rain slink behind me. Rain says that gopher-ing for Ten Bears was the worst day of his life, even worse than the Halloween his mom dressed him up as a lemon yellow sea urchin.

"Where's Snow?"

"Who's Snow?"

"C'mon, Ten Bears. You know who I mean. Gopher Girl."

"Hey, Dip." Snow to the rescue. She crosses the corral in full cowgirl gear. "And hey to you, Mister Ten Bears."

Ten Bears frowns, having lost his chance to mess with us.

Snow whispers, "Follow me to Wishing Rock."

Wishing Rock is a nearby sandstone ledge that juts over a bottle-green pond. Rain and I dangle our feet in the water while Snow digs a crumpled sheet of paper out of her pocket.

"This is the letter my dad discovered in an old lady's trunk. It's the real thing."

"So Butch wrote it, huh?"

"And sent it to Kid Curry, one of The Wild Bunch."

My BlackBerry vibrates but I ignore it. "No signature ... how's your dad sure that Butch wrote it - "

" my dad is *the* full service Butch Cassidy expert, right down to the handwriting."

Rain skips ahead. "What's the big deal here? This is just chitchat about cattle rustling and mining camps."

"There's more. Check out the last three lines."

Kid, when you've surved your time and ar free
And lookin for your share of the Inka jewelry
You'll find it buried by cedar -----

"I can't see the last word," says Rain. "It's smudged out."

Snow hesitates, takes a deep breath and goes for it. "This is what my dad thinks.

"Butch's last heist was a hoard of gold jewelry. Kid Curry was in on the robbery but got tossed in the clink before he got his. Dad says Butch wrote the letter to tell the Kid where his share was buried. See, the Kid was a head case who'd gun down folks for nothing. Butch sure didn't want to get him angry."

"Did the Kid ever get his share?"

"No. He got shot in a jailbreak first."

"So what happened to - "

" - good question. Dad thinks it's still here."

"Ha! So that's what Tweedledee and Tweedledum are digging for: Butch's last score!"

"You got it. C'mon, let's get back to the stables before Ten Bears throws a fit."

I mention a story I heard from our waiter at the lodge. "What's this myth about Wishing Rock? Is that just something you Locals tell the *turistas*?"

Snow shakes her head and the pale blonde hair falls out of her baseball cap. "No, it's the real deal. A Local who touches Wishing Rock gets one wish, although it never comes true like they expect."

Her mention of Locals stops me dead in my tracks.

"I'm Local at home but not here. Can I still wish?"

"You can try. Just don't tell anyone."

I rub my hand on Wishing Rock and make a secret wish: *Just once I want to see Big Dip like he used to be.*

Right then my BlackBerry vibrates.

14
Cedar ?

I'm so sick of strange texts from strange people that I flip off my BlackBerry without looking. Rain and I launch a righteous boarding session and don't return to the lodge 'til dinner. We find my dad slumped in an overstuffed chair outside the dining room. I'm used to seeing him all business so it's odd to see him all worn-out.

Rain and I take chairs sandwiching him.

"What's up, dad?"

"Yeah, what's happening, Mr. L?"

"My Denver trip was a bust. I traveled all day for nothing. I'm still stumped about what's going on."

It's a downer to see dad like this. Not only does he usually have all the answers, he's got more answers than there are questions. Lucky for him I'm on the job.

"Rain and I know what the pit-diggers want."

Dad pops up and swivels his head. "Whatcha mean?"

I hand over Butch's letter and dad scans it eagerly.

"This is rustler talk."

"That's what we thought at first. But Snow says the last three lines are the clue to where Butch buried the treasure that Romo and Fumi want."

Dad frowns. "Why's a legit professor hanging around with creeps like Fomo and Rumi, anyway?"

"That's *Romo* and *Fumi*," puts in Rain.

"We're not sure about the connection, dad. Any chance the Super can arrest Romo - "

" - for what? There's no proof he did anything wrong. You have to catch him - I mean, the *police* have to catch him - in the act." Dad yawns. "In the meantime, *I* need a nap."

I turn to Rain. "This is scary. Dad is getting seriously" - I'm embarrassed to say it – "*old*."

Rain nods gravely like a doctor consulting on a terminal patient. "Yeah, looks that way."

Scary. As much as my dad bugs me, I never want him to get ... *old*.

"Rainbow Man, dig out your i-phone. There's detecting to do and my Blackberry's low on juice."

"Don't you ever take a break, Mr. Junior Detective?"

"No. Let's search for an outlaw blog."

"Outlaw blog? I'll bet a million bucks there's no such thing."

Lucky he doesn't have a million bucks cuz if he did he'd lose it. There's not one outlaw blog, there're dozens.

"Who knew the world was full of outlaw freaks?"

It turns out outlaw freaks peddle the same oddball trinkets as cowboy freaks. Outlaw beer mugs, poker chips, blankets, chairs, gambling chips, dishes, diaries, replicas of six-shooters and bronzed imitation cowboy boots. We sort through the rubbish and click on the chat room Stickemup.com. I leave a post:

> *Anyone with info about Butch and cedar - ?, please contact the Wild West Skateboarders.*

"OK, that took all of sixty seconds. Now what?" says Rain.

Good question. For some odd reason, I wonder what Fern Randall would do.

Huh? Did *I* say that? I must be losing it. Fern's made my life miserable since pre-school. She shoots up her hand when I can't answer a question and she's always right. Then she smiles a goofy smile as if she squashed a bug. Me.

Rain reads my face. "Looks like you saw a ghost."

"Scarier. I was inside Fern Randall's head."

"Whoa, weird." But Rain's intrigued. "You mean like, what'd she do if she were us ... hmm? Yeah, she always knows what to do ... at least she acts like it."

"She'd keep digging, Rain. Fern *never* gives up. Like, she hasn't given up bugging me and she's been doing it ten years already." I have to admit, Fern's determination impresses me.

"Read the poem again, wouldja?"

Rain screws up his face and his eyebrows knit tight.

Kid, when you've surved your time and ar free
And lookin for your share of the Inka jewelry
You'll find it buried by cedar -----

"Shoot. Just one word. *Knees ... free ... spree*?"
Then it comes to me. "*Trees* ... cedar *trees*! That's it!
Romo and Fumi are digging by *cedar trees*!"

Later I get the nagging feeling that maybe the answer came too easily. Cedar *trees*? Maybe. Anyway, right now I'm excited.

My BlackBerry buzzes with another Private Call. Rain reads the text.

MEET AT RIM TRAIL + ZION NARROWS. NOW. SNO.

"No can do," says Rain uneasily. "The ranger said there's a thunderstorm warning and hikers should stay off the trails cuz the canyon can flashflood."

On cue there's a long rumble of thunder and the sky turns black and purple. Rain's eyebrows knit like my dad's when he's in fun vacuum mode. Why's everyone going un-fun on me?

"That stupid storm's a long way away. We can't sit around doing nothing, letting a bit of weather stop us. If you don't grab at things they won't happen."

Before Rain comes up with a good answer, I grab the park map, grab his arm and grab the up-canyon shuttle to the mouth of Zion Narrows.

15

Slot Canyon

Lucky for us the shuttle comes right away. Seems lucky at the time, anyway.

"No itty-bitty thunderstorm stops *us*," I boast. "So what if it's a slot canyon? We *Nuevos* don't back down for stupid warnings."

I don't feel so fearless once I settle in my shuttle seat. To be honest, I'm homesick. I miss my mom's spaghetti and meatballs, I miss Big Dip and I'm tired of red rocks and sagebrush. I miss the ocean. I want to kick Romo's butt but ... I want to go home. This weird Wild West stuff couldn't happen back home.

Rain fiddles with his i-phone as our shuttle bus lumbers up the canyon to Zion Narrows.

"What's up, RainMan?"

"I logged in to WesternMemorabilia.Dealers.com. Guess who hails from Santa Monica, California besides us?"

"Butch Cassidy IV?"

"Good guess but no banana. Romo Cosezu and his brother Fumi, that's who. They call themselves The Wild West Brothers and their office is at Bicknell and Main."

"A block from Bicknell Hill? I don't believe it."

"See for yourself."

Rain hands me the i-phone and sure enough, Romo and Fumi are striking a geek pose in front of The Galley restaurant.

"The website says they brokered a Kit Carson letter for $500,000. These bozos don't mess with small potatoes."

"What's the prof's angle? I didn't take him for a greed merchant."

"Snow's cool, but let's face it, her dad is sketch."

True enough. Actually, he's more than sketch. He's most of the way down the road to full-on shaky.

The shuttle grinds to a stop at Zion Narrows trailhead. We're the only ones who get off and we see a sign that says:

BEWARE FLASH FLOOD ZONE!
OBTAIN WEATHER FORECAST
BEFORE HIKING

Rain frowns.

"That's for the stupid *turistas*," I mutter.

When the first raindrops fall, I say, "No biggie."

"Strange place to meet," complains Rain. "In the middle of nowhere. Maybe *we're* the stupid *turistas* in this picture."

"Not a chance," I reply. But I'm thinking the same thing. Why'd Snow choose *here*?

We wade in and slog upstream. With each step our sneakers slip and slide off the rocky bottom. The water's only a foot deep but the current is ferocious.

"Think we're close?"

"Text her again."

"No luck." I seal my BlackBerry back in a plastic bag as it vibrates with another message.

"It's that same goofy text: DIP, WHERE R U?"

"You attract some real whack jobs," smirks Rain.

"Yeah, like you!"

Shivering, we trudge upstream until the canyon narrows to six feet wide. There's no one but us.

""I got a bad feeling she's not coming," says Rain.

"Hmm ... maybe the sneak brothers pulled a fast one - "

" - look ahead!" shouts Rain.

I whip my head around to see a wall of water rushing around the river bend two hundred yards upstream.

"Up the cliff! It's our only chance!"

Frantically, Rain and I scramble up the steep canyon side. We're fifteen feet up when the wall of water rumbles beneath us. We climb ten more feet and stop, a couple of surf rats scared of water for the first time.

16

COWBOYLOVER

"You say a girl named Snow lured you up a slot canyon into a flashflood?" My dad's ears could pass for purple glow sticks.

"There's another explanation," I insist defensively. "She wouldn't do that intentionally."

"So who texted you if not her?"

"Not sure." I feel like a moron admitting that I got suckered by a phony text. Not to mention that I dragged Rain into it.

"Mr. L, we thought it was Snow but now we don't. We learned our lesson and won't do it again." Trust Rain to know how to play my dad.

If I forgot to mention, Rain and I are plastered in bandages thanks to a nurse in Super Sandy's office. We had to wait hours for the flood to recede before we came down from our perch. But it wasn't bad once we knew for sure we'd make it. Like surfing a storm swell, getting sucked under and popping up to do it again.

Now the sun's out and the sky's bright blue like a crayon. The Super opens his office windows and the warm Utah air rushes in. It's good to be dry even if I'm still chilled knowing there's a certain someone out to get me. I've gotten under that certain someone's skin. A certain beaky someone.

"Listen, Dip." The Super lays a hand on my shoulder and looks me in the eye. Not easy since he's five inches shorter than me. "We appreciate your help but this situation has taken a turn for the worse. It's time to let the adults take over."

"My thought exactly," says dad. "You kids have done your bit."

Kids? Bit?

"I won't quit 'til we catch who set us up. I want payback."

Not a smart thing to say. My dad and the Super trade worried looks as if afraid I'll jump off the nearest deep end.

Well, maybe I will.

"Dip's just talking big," puts in Rain. ""We'll be careful. Extra-extra careful."

Dad hesitates. "Hmm ... you grab a bite while I make some calls. Stick close to the lodge, OK?"

"Sure, Mr. L," says Rain.

I swallow the urge to keep bugging my dad and instead accompany Rain to the snack bar for our seventh pineapple pizza of the trip. "Now that we've got some privacy, log on - "

" - I know, I know," says Rain, "Stickmeup.com."

Seconds later, we're checking posts to the Wild West Skateboarders (that's us) in my new favorite chat room. Bingo! A mystery blogger named COWBOYLOVER has sent this:

IT'S CEDAR LEIGH YOU WANT.

"Huh? *Cedar Leigh*?"
"Hmm. Plug *Cedar Leigh* in the poem."

Kid, when you've surved your time and ar free
And lookin for your share of the Inka jewelry
You'll find it buried by **Cedar Leigh**

106

"Whoa! That fits! But what's a Cedar Leigh?"

"Ask COWBOYLOVER. Meanwhile, I've got a second bright idea: squeeze the beakies until they admit they sent the fake text."

Rain looks queasy. "I've got a bright idea. Let's not and say we did."

Geez. Sometimes I think I'm the only one who knows how to have fun.

17
Pack Up And Go Home

Rain and dad must be secretly conspiring against me cuz after we've eaten dad announces he's got his own bright idea.

"Time to get you out of trouble."

"Geez, dad, technically, going home isn't staying out of trouble ... it's running away from trouble - "

" - time you pack up, Dip. I mean it."

"You can't be serious. I'm not leaving until I give Romo a custom beak job, no charge."

"That's why we're leaving before you get killed," says dad. "I've already got explaining to do how I let you get conked out by a shovel." He grins sheepishly. "Didja know Big Dip misses ... *you*?"

And I miss him. Maybe I forgot to mention that I made sure he'd be OK while I was gone by putting Duane in charge of search and rescue. Might seem strange I chose Duane cuz we don't always get along that good and teachers at school say he's a goofy truant. What they don't know is that Duane skips school cuz he takes care of his sick mom in a spare room above Comet Liquor and works five nights a week in the stockroom.

Funny how the stuff teachers should know they never do.

"I'll give you credit for ID-ing the vandals, " admits dad. "But there's not enough evidence to arrest them. It's just your word against theirs."

"The sheriff could - "

" - Sheriff Shackle paid a visit to the Cone ranch and the prof refused to answer any questions. FYI, I checked him out with a real history expert in Denver. Cone has a rep as a loose cannon who gets his facts wrong."

"But I need to say goodbye to Snow."

"No, it's a long drive as it is."

Running out on Snow feels crummy. It doesn't make it any better that as I'm packing stuff in the car my dad is lobbing out advice about space utilization. Like, it's news that the soft stuff goes in the corners? Anyway, as consolation dad agrees we can stop on the way at Butch Cassidy's childhood home.

I lie back against the headrest and let things happen as our Volvo slides out the park exit, speeds through a mile-long tunnel and heads for the remains of Circleville, Utah. Soon we're shooting footage of the one-room shack where Butch grew up. Hard to believe it but the Old West's most famous outlaw grew up in the frontier equivalent of a cardboard box.

A beater pickup rolls up next to us and a sunburned gaffer limps out. He seems cheery enough although he looks like he's fallen off one horse too many. Maybe Ten Bears is right that you'll never be a cowboy if you're too afraid of being thrown.

"I'll betcha you fans of Butch Cassidy."

"Yessiree," says dad. "Big fans."

"You and the rest of the world. *Turistas* hunt and peck for souvenirs no matter how I try to stop 'em. Just last week I caught two strange birds digging by the cedars and hadda fill 'em up myself. The holes, that is, not the fellas. Heh, heh."

"What did you - "

" - name's Marlin," says the gaffer. "And the looky-lous show up everyday. Most are nice enough. It's just the greedy ones who steal everything not nailed down.

"Yep," he continues, "wouldja believe it? Two fellers with big noses. Sassed me with a fishy story about why they's here." Marlin sniffs. "Made no sense. Told 'em to shove."

"Get their names?"

"Saw no need when they skedaddled."

"What'd they look like?"

"Don't rightly know. Couldn't see past their noses. Burned bright red they was. Told 'em to scoot or I'd fetch my shotgun."

I hiss excitedly. "Romo and Fumi ... digging by *cedar trees*."

Rain can't hear me. He's got his ear buds in and his head's bobbing up and down like a piston.

"Think they found what they wanted?"

"Nah. They was in an ugly mood when they shoved. But listen to this. Some jokers had the nerve to dig up the graves of Butch's parents. Town had to cap 'em with cement. You might say there's been a whole lotta digging going on!"

My dad thinks that's funny.

From there, I nap on the way to Baker and the giant thermometer, where we eat dinner at the Mad Greek. I drop back in an uneasy half-doze, bummed to be leaving Zion with the mystery unsolved and heading for a confrontation with fat Kyle and his brother.

My BlackBerry buzzes.

GLAD UR COMING HOME.

18
Warst Is The Worst

Next morning I'm in school and it's like I never left. I'm milling around with the inmates outside the prison cell known as Smart Teenagers Making Smart Choices, while warden J.W. Warst licks his chops, hoping I'll screw up. He wants to humiliate me for the 167th time this year.

In the precious few minutes of freedom before class, if you have something to say you better sound off loud and clear. Either that or accept being an extra in the Kyle Gibson-Stacy Peach show. Sure enough, right on schedule Kyle starts bragging about his spring break ski trip to Mammoth. I'm tempted to ask how he managed to ski with a bum knee but I keep that can of worms unopened for the moment. Anyway, Kyle says that his ski instructor told his *advanced* class that Mammoth has the best snow in all of California. Stacy butts in and brags that *her* ski instructor at *Vail* told her *expert* class that Vail powder is the best in the entire *world*.

If anyone else went skiing over spring break they're smart enough to shut up about it. No one wants a bragging war with Kyle or The Peach.

Duane fills me in on what went down at the beach.

"Dig this, a posse of Vals wiped out on the hill. Bam-bam. One lame-o broke his foot and another broke his wrist. We sent 'em back to the Valley in an ambulance. Ha, ha."

Kyle lasers in on me. "What'd The Flakeboard King do on his break? Chase his loony grandpa around the Promenade?"

Everybody tenses, waiting to see if I'll let Kyle get away with that. The Peach breaks it up by saying, "Kyle, that's pathetic."

Mr. W waves us in class, steering us to our seats like a bunch of five year-olds.

Duane hisses, "Why'd you let Kyle put down your grandpa?"

I hiss, "I've got to cool the fighting."

Maybe I didn't mention it before, but I get in too many fights. Fights on the beach and in the park. Fights with boys I knew and boys I didn't. When I was small even mom liked that I stuck up for myself. Now I'm older she tells me to cool it. But how can I when the world is full of Kyle Gibsons?

Yet I ignore Kyle's taunt for the moment.

"Good morning, people," chirps Mr. W, sounding like a plastic toy with fresh batteries.

"Hey, Mr. W," a few toadies reply. Fern is one of them.

If you ask me, the highlight of Mr. W's day is figuring out a way to torture me. Today is no different. He rubs his newly bleached buzz cut as his eyes glow behind his bug-shaped glasses. It's enough to make me throw up.

"It's Monday, people. You know what that means. Mock Theater! Who wants to kick us off after spring break?"

Silence. Even the dullest knife in the drawer knows to fly under Mr. W's radar.

"Ahhh!" He spins around. "Mr. Gibson."

Kyle frowns.

"Front and center, please."

Kyle angrily limps to the front and I'm pleased to see a blue knee brace peek out from a hole in his jeans. So much for the *advanced* skiing.

Mr. W spins around. "And ... *Mr. Little!*"

I knew it. Mr. W heard how I kicked in Kyle's knee.

"For you newcomers, Mock Theater is a safe zone where sincere teenagers resolve their differences in an atmosphere of mutual respect. Mr. Gibson, Mr. Little ... shall we begin?"

Ugh. Mock Theater makes me want to kick in Warst's knee too. The class holds its breath, happy for another Dip v. Kyle showdown.

"Let's set the stage." Warst clears his throat. "Mr. Gibson and Mr. Little want to take the same girl to Spring Fling. Let's have, oh let's say, Miss Peach plays the girl. C'mon, people, get in the swing."

It's no stretch for The Peach to get in the swing of boys fighting over her. She's a professional eye-batter and hair-player-with. But something inside me makes me blurt, "I won't play your stupid Mock Theater."

Did I say that?

"You don't have a choice," Mr. W snaps. "This is school, not a skateboard trick in a parking lot."

"I wish a cute boy invited me to the dance," purrs The Peach. She flicks her eyes back and forth between me and Kyle.

Mr. W nods. He was right to choose her to get things going!

"I won't play," I repeat.

The class oohs and aahs as Mr. W does the headshaking thing. "How about you, Mr. Gibson, are you a team player?"

"Sure," I snap. "He's a jackass too."

I gotta hand it to Kyle. For a big lunk he's fast. He nails me in the chest before I get my hands up. I didn't figure him for the guts to do that in front of Warst.

My resolve not to fight flashes through my mind, but if I back off Kyle will never lay off me. So I launch a sidekick. I miss Kyle completely and fall on my face. I said I was fast, not smooth.

Kyle belly-flops on me like the Masked Fatman in a wrestling show. He knocks the wind out of me and gets up to do it again when Mr. W gets in between us. Bad idea.

Kyle flattens *him* instead of me. To add insult to injury, Kyle's desk tips over and pins Mr. W down.

The class jumps to its feet and cheers for the first time in Mock Theater history.   Thirty-two pairs of fists pump in the air and thirty-two voices chant, "More, more, more!"

The door flies open and Murph the campus rent-a-cop rushes in to get Mr. W out from under the desk. Warst is so green that Murph has to make him lie down and wait for an ambulance. When Murph shakes his head I figure he's shaking it at me like everyone else does, until I realize he's actually shaking it at the quivering jelly-like teacher who just vomited on the classroom floor.

19
Taking Charge

You probably already figured out I'd pay a price. First, Principal Tenzer spends his lunch hour telling me off. Then he calls my dad and my dad tells me off for another hour. He throws in the headshaking thing for free. When dad's neck gets tired, he drops me off at home with strict instructions not to leave the house. Needless to say, soon as he's gone I sneak out to the beach.

Big Dip is on the Bay Street seawall and I sink down beside him to fill him in. He guffaws when he hears how Mr. W's class has been redubbed, Dumb Teenagers Making Bad Choices.

And that's by Principal Tenzer.

"Thanks for taking my side. But you know that M&D are on my case. They say I get in too much trouble."

"You've got spunk, Dipfield."

"*Spunk*? That's serious old fogey lingo, grandpa."

"So call it *energy*."

"Hmm ... what if M&D are right that I should change?"

"Oh?" Big Dip arches his eyebrows to indicate that for me to change will be as easy as turning into a jackrabbit. "Do *you* want to change?"

"Naah, but I'm sick of getting in trouble."

My BlackBerry vibrates. It's Snow. One look at my face and Big Dip knows to give me space. "Hey, Snow, how's school?"

"Same old same old. Riding the bus twenty-five miles each way with a bunch of yokels. Sure wish you were here."

"What's up with the Beaky Brothers?"

"More same old. Still bugging my dad."

"Why doesn't he kick them to the curb?"

"They have something on him. They hustled him away last night and he didn't come home for hours." She muffles her voice. "This morning his clothes were in the washer, covered with mud.

"Any chance you can come, Dip?"

"Not yet. My dad's putting together a paper trail of Romo and Fumi's deals. When he's done we'll come. Meanwhile, the Super's on the lookout for new digs but

Zion's so big he probably won't catch the beakies in the act." I hesitate. "Is your dad in on it?"

"I didn't want to believe it but ... yeah, probably." Snow sighs. "Romo is destroying dad's life and mine - "

" – I'm working a lead but I can't tell you," I say, trying to make her feel better. "I'll get back to you when my plan's set."

My lead? COWBOYLOVER. Some lead. At least it gives her hope.

"Stay in touch, Dip?"

"Of course."

I check the outlaw blog but there's no reply from COWBOYLOVER on, what's a *Cedar Leigh?* Some questions are like that, don't you think? You gotta sit back and wait for the answer.

Better get back to the house before M&D check on me.

20
Last Sail

In Zion I was free to spend as much time as I wanted on the pit mystery. But at home I've got other fish to fry too. There's that matter of my nine to three at school and I've got homework on top of that. Today it's Life Sciences. I'm supposed to contrast the theories of evolution and creationism.

The assignment warns in bold that:

Remember! This essay counts for 20% of your grade!

Fifteen minutes race by after I'm home and all I managed to do is type my name at the top of the page. Good start. At this rate I'll finish that essay in, oh, maybe twenty years.

I stare across the bay at the Malibu hills ten miles away. Why aren't I out there on the vast deep Pacific? I could sail past Point Dume and never look back. No parents. No rules.

No wonder Big Dip loves to sail.

I return to my essay. Fifteen more minutes pass and I've only written half a sentence.

The theory of evolution is ...

Is what, exactly? I'm tempted to say that it's one of those things that you assume you know what it you really don't.

I mean, like am *I* the product of evolution? A hundred thousand years ago was there a 1.0 version of me chirping happily as I dragged around my long hairy arms looking for nuts? Did I have a long hairy-armed archenemy named Kyle Gibson? Did I kick the 1.0 Kyle in the knee to keep him in line?

Hmm.

Maybe the old me had a buddy named Cro-Rainbow Man. Maybe there was a Cro-Stacy-Peach, with long thin arms and pink nail polish on the tips of her hairy fingers.

If that's so, then we haven't evolved much since then, cuz evolution is supposed to make us advance us, right? But I'm not stupid enough to run a smart-alec answer like that up the flagpole with Mr. Gomez. He's not one of those smart-alecs-are-cute teachers.

I decide I'll return to the essay later. Now I deserve to go down to the kitchen for a snack. I've begun mowing through a pile of Oreos when Big Dip wanders in and snags a handful for himself. He's wearing an old pair of Top Siders and his favorite sailing jersey. *Sail or Die*. We're eating cookies at the counter when my BlackBerry buzzes.

It's Big Dip! He's texting me from three feet away. He's got Jesse's BlackBerry and he's smiling from ear to ear.

PLZ SAL WITH ME.

Not bad for a first time texter.

"Your sailing days are over, grandpa. You said so yourself."

"I've got one more sail in me. C'mon along."

My eyes flick to the empty chairs in the living room where my parents usually sit.

"Gotta clear it with M&D first."

"No, I asked *you*. I'm eighty years old, for heaven's sakes. I don't need to clear things with your M&D."

"But we don't own a boat, grandpa."

"I called and we can rent one at the pier."

"It'll get dark soon."

"We won't go very far. We'll be back before you know it."

I'm weakening. Geez, I wish M&D were at home to deal with this. Then again maybe I don't. They'd pull the plug for sure but I don't want to. I always wanted to sail with Big Dip.

"Let's do it."

Big Dip jumps to his feet and struts out the door. Ten minutes later we're at the pier, where he whips out his Visa card at Sammy's Boats and rents us a mini version of The Big Dipper. We climb in and push off.

"Uh, I gotta remind you I never sailed before. If we get in trouble I won't know what to do."

"You, afraid of trouble? I don't believe it."

I man the jib and Big Dip handles the mainsail. He steers toward our house while telling me the story of his first sail seventy years ago. Nothing wrong with his memory now.

It seems that when Big Dip was eight and his brother was five, they hijacked their uncle's sailboat in Christmas Cove, Maine. They didn't know how to sail and immediately got blown out to the open Atlantic. Lucky for them, Big Dip's dad chased them down in a dory.

Wow, says Big Dip with a grin, did we catch hell! And it was all my fault! He beams with pleasure. I try to imagine him as a boy. Yeah, I'm starting to see it.

A breeze drives our boat scudding across the water and Big Dip glows like a light bulb turned on in his head. I'm happy to see him happy. Makes me feel better about the lecture I'm bound to get from M&D when we get home.

"This is the spot," he says, when we're offshore our house. He luffs the mainsail and the boat rocks.

"This is nowheresville. It's *home*. My bedroom is fifty yards away."

Big Dip trails a hand in the bottle-green water. "This is it."

"Okay, grandpa, I bite. What's it?"

"This is where I want you to put me when it's time."

Now I get it. He wants his ashes spread here when he dies.

"That won't happen for a long time ... I don't want to think about it ... and I don't want you to go."

"I don't want to leave but I will. Sooner than you think."

"M&D will plant you in that old cemetery in Massachusetts. Dad says that all the Littles get planted there."

Big Dip's blue eyes glint. "I won't go. I hate cold winters and I want to stay with *you*."

I'm tempted to say the obvious. He won't have a choice where he goes when he's dead and he won't be cold either. But I keep that to myself.

"Make darn sure I stay here, Dip. I'm counting on you."

"Clear it with M&D. They won't do anything *I* say."

"It's *you* I trust." Big Dip's voice softens. "It's a gift to be trusted ... it's OK to be scared."

That stings. Me, scared?

OK, so maybe I am. What of it? I'm scared of his leaving and I'm not so crazy about his so-called gift, either.

Besides, there's nothing special about the spot he chose. Sure, for a moment the ocean had glistened and a handful of gulls swooped and cawed as if to invite him to fly up and join them. But just as quickly the light changed and the birds flew away and the ocean turned murky and foreboding.

"You grab at life, grandson. So did I. Your dad ... he's a planner. He works out life in advance. You and me, we jump in and swim even if we don't know the right direction.

"Don't we ... *Dip*."

He raises the mainsail and we tack back to the pier. It takes a moment for it to sink in that he called me ... *Dip*.

21
New Clue

Big Dip and I get home to find Rain on our stoop.

"Dude, your mom's got spaghetti and meatballs for dinner! We're waiting on you guys."

My mom's number one specialty is spaghetti and meatballs. Rain hasn't missed it in years. His own mom is a tofu Trojan who sticks it in everything from Gatorade to oatmeal. No *Nuevo* with half a brain drops in on Rain for dinner.

By the way, if I didn't mention it, I've had the funny feeling that we've been followed home from the pier. I glance over my shoulder before going inside and yeah, I'm right. It's that shrimp skateboarder who hangs around Bicknell Hill buddying up to me. Grody something or other.

"What's that gremmie's name?" I ask Rain.

"Albright," says Rain. "Grody Albright."

"You mean, as in *Freddy Albright*?"

Freddy is the *uber* nerd of John Adams Middle School.

"It's his little bro. He's not like Freddy."

Freddy Albright brings to school the most awesome lunches ever. Roast beef sandwiches, chocolate cake *and* brownies. Even French Fries that he heats up in a solar powered French Fry box. Naturally, everyone except Kyle Gibson is eager to trade lunches. Not Kyle. He doesn't trade, he just steals Freddy's lunch by threatening to kick his butt.

One time Rain won Freddy's lunch by winning a bet about a biology question that Freddy thought Rain wouldn't know. Freddy figured Rain and me for stupid skaters. He lost a monster BBQ beef sandwich making that mistake.

So why's his little bro dogging *me*?

"C'mon in. Time to eat."

Mom dishes up spaghetti with one hand and pats Big Dip on the head with the other. Meanwhile she carries on a conversation with Jesse's new boyfriend, a guy so dumb he makes her ex-boyfriend Chopper seem smart. Jesse is busy texting. Probably to Chopper.

Dad's got his headset on and he's reviewing some figures from a national park super halfway across the country. Another day, another park, another problem.

In other words, a typical Wednesday at the Little house. It's the only night of the week we sit down for dinner and we still end up doing our own thing.

Mom glances at my still full plate and frowns. She's sensitive about her cooking. "You haven't eaten a bite and it's your favorite meal." She turns to Big Dip. "You haven't either."

Big Dip and I grin at each other. We pigged out on corndogs and orange slush at Hot Dog On A Stick. I swallow a corndog burp and ask if Rain and I can be excused to do our homework. Mom raises her eyebrows as if to say, yeah sure, now I've heard everything, but nods.

Up in my room, Rain and I log on to Stickmeup.com for any news from COWBOYLOVER.

"Check it out, Rain. He got back to us."

CEDAR LEIGH WAS BUTCH'S
HORSE.
LOOK FOR HIM IN GRAFTON.

"That cinches it. You and me are going to Grafton. Wherever it is."

"Forget Grafton. We're home and staying home."

"Aww, Rain. We're back on the case."

Rain whistles. "Is this a contest between you and your dad? One of those father-son generational-competition-struggle things?"

"What are you babbling about, dude?"

"You're competing with him, aren't you," says Rain, his eyebrows lifted as if it never occurred to him. "Didja know that?"

"This isn't amateur shrink hour, Rain. Log on the JAMS website, for Pedro's sake."

On our middle school website the homework blog is run by, who else, Fern Randall. Her regular feature is, **Ask Fern!** You email in your hardest homework and she does it in sixty seconds or less, timing herself with an online stopwatch.

The gossip blog is, **The Peach Report,** Stacy's torture chamber for wannabe poppies. She blabs about the wild and crazy stuff she's doing and the AWESOME people she's met and by the time you finish reading you're guaranteed to feel three inches tall.

Tonight's subject is none other than ... Rain
Bowman and yours truly, Little Dip.

WHERE WERE TWO OF OUR OWN JAMS
SKATERS
OVER SPRING BREAK?
WHY, IN UTAH!
WHEREVER THAT IS
MEANWHILE, YOUR REPORTER WAS A
SPECIAL
GUEST AT THE HOTTEST TEEN CLUB IN
HOLLYWOOD
GUESS WHO I SAW?
MORE IMPORTANT, GUESS WHO SAW ME?!

"Rain, log off that stupid blog before I throw up.
Jump on MapQuest and locate Grafton."

"OK, boss."

Rain clicks and scrolls halfway to forever before
shoving the mouse away in defeat. "No matter how tight I
zoom in on Google Earth, Grafton's just a dot on the map."

"Whatcha mean?"

"Grafton doesn't have any roads or homes. No schools or streets or parks. Not a single building. It's as if nobody lives there!"

22
The Dream

After Rain leaves for home I return to my Life Sciences homework. Here's how I wind up my description of evolution:

The theory of evolution is ... a joke since thousands of years later you still end up with ape-men like Kyle Gibson.

Hmmm ... that won't fly with Mr. Gomez. I delete it and buckle down to work for fifteen minutes before logging on to GameHouse to play Collapse! II, Pop and Drop, TextTwist and Knock 'em Out 'til midnight. I'll take another crack at that evolution business tomorrow.

Then I go to sleep and dream. In my dream, Big Dip and I are sailing on his sloop, The Big Dipper, but instead of sailing on water we're skimming over thick Zion sand. Stacy and Snow board our boat and push-pull me back and forth between them.

Snow: He's mine.

Stacy: I can have him back whenever I want.

Snow: No, you can't.

Stacy: Wanna bet?

Snow throws Stacy overboard and she makes a splash. In *sand*?

Then I'm standing at the head of the class in Life Sciences. Mr. Gomez has called on me to explain the theory of evolution and I'm going to use Stacy and Snow as examples. But is it Stacy who evolved into Snow or the other way around?

Then I'm back in the Big Dipper, only this time it's with Butch Cassidy. We're two outlaws on the run and a team of ponies struggles furiously to pull us through the deep sand.

I pop up in bed, wide-awake. A grayish light filters in my windows and from my computer I text COWBOYLOVER to ask where's Grafton. He surprises me by texting right back.

GRAFTON'S A DOT ON THE MAP CUZ NO ONE'S LIVED THERE FOR A HUNDRED YEARS. IT'S A GHOST TOWN.

Ah! A shiver goes up and down my spine. Ghost town? Too cool for words. Now I have the final puzzle piece. I know who's Cedar Leigh and where's Grafton and what the Beaky Brothers want. All that's left is to tie it up with a ribbon and a bow and present it to my dad.

My BlackBerry shimmies with a text from Snow.

THINGS R BAD. CAN U COME?

What timing! I text back.

WILL B ZION TODAY.

Now what?

I wake Rain on his I-phone. "We're going to Zion, like it or not."

"You gotta be kidding. Just how are *you* getting there?"

"Me? You mean, how are *we* getting there?"

"Your M&D on board with this?"

"Uhh ... not exactly."

"No plan, no permission ... no way. Let the Super handle it."

"Don't make this a big deal. You and me always do stuff we're not supposed to."

"Don't remind me. Remember the last time?"

"You mean boarding down Wilshire Boulevard at two in the morning? It was just bad luck that the police happened to - "

" - no, although come to think of it - "

" - Topanga Canyon? How was I supposed to know your wheels would fall off? That'll teach you to buy cheap plastic - "

" - hey, I'd forgotten that - "

" - or d'ya mean the time we let the air out of Warst's tires?"

"No! I mean the jellyfish!"

Yeah I remember. OK, so maybe I should've mentioned that the lifeguard said no surfing 'til the jellyfish cleared out. How was I supposed to know Rain would get stung you-know-where?

"I've got something better to do tomorrow anyway."

"Better than Zion?"

"I'm teaching Brandy Southwait how to surf - "

" - Brandy? She'll burn you, Rain, she's too hot for you - "

Actually I'm jealous. Brandy's cool.

" - take my advice and stay home. Dip. This could be your biggest crash and burn ever. You're going AWOL, and I don't mean, Always West Of Lincoln."

" Don't flake out on me - "

" - later." Rain hangs up.

I kick back in bed. Overhead on the ceiling are the glow stars that my dad stuck up when I was two years old. Until this moment I forgot they were there. I'm like that. Sometimes I forget what's right in front of me.

Not in a million years will M&D let me skip school to go to Zion, not after my latest snafu. Even though it wasn't my fault. How was I supposed to know Mr. W would break his ankle?

If dad thinks Zion's not my mystery he's wrong. He got me into it and he can't turn me off 'til I say so.

All of a sudden it hits me how I'll get to Zion.

23
Going AWOL

I tiptoe downstairs and knock on Big Dip's bedroom door. He listens carefully and nods.

"Sure, I'll take you to Zion. After all, I asked you a bigger favor. Matter of fact, I say we leave right now."

"Really?" I'm a bit surprised he's going for it. I guess he's let go of that can't-do-it attitude that keeps the average adult down.

"I say we slip out before you-know-who wake up."

"You mean ... M&D?"

"Yep, Team Fun Vacuum. If they catch wind of what we've got in mind they'll squash us like a couple of potato bugs."

"Yeah. No way they'll let me cut school. You know dad's motto: *Follow your dreams and you'll end up with nightmares.*"

Big Dip laughs. "That's your dad. We couldn't convince him there's no mail on Sunday." Big Dip pulls out his Visa card. "I may be old but I've got dough. Call a cab, we've got a flight to catch."

Next thing I know I'm buying two tickets at LAX and texting Snow that we're on our way. I don't text Rain. The less he knows the better. And definitely not M&D. Big Dip and I are flying under the radar on this one.

After we land in Vegas, we board a small puddle-jumper for the flight to St. George, where Big Dip puts his Visa card to work and rents us a VW Bug for the drive to the park. By the time we reach Springdale he's bushed. His bright blue eyes have sunk into his pale, lined face.

"Take it from here, wouldja."

I say, "There's that little matter of a driver's license -
"

" - I'm sick of other people's rules," he says. "Aren't you?"

Can't argue with that.

" - so hit it, grandson."

I weave us through a sluggish wagon train of RV's and *turista* sightseeing buses. Horns honk wildly when I cut off a bread van by mistake. But we reach the park in one piece and Big Dip doesn't complain once.

At the lodge, he checks us in while I fetch him a roast beef sandwich and an extra blanket. Soon as we get to our room he flops on the bed and I cover him. In seconds he's snoring, looking like he could sleep forever.

Maybe asking him to come was selfish, but it feels right to have him along. This is a double Dip adventure I couldn't have with M&D.

My BlackBerry does its dance. Snow.

MEET ME PIZZA FACTORY AT 6.
GETTING BAD. B CAREFUL.

Hmm. My watch says 5:15. Better hustle.

Even though I'm in a hurry I decide not to take the Bug. Last thing I need is to get pulled over by a cop before I meet Snow.   So I hightail it to the shuttle stop and catch the bus in to town. There's only one other small problem ... what to do about the dozen messages from M&D?

Where are you? Is Big Dip OK? Come home NOW!!!

Don't shake your head at me that it's unfair to keep M&D in the dark. There's no way I'm giving away what I'm up to by calling back.

The shuttle drops me at the Pizza Factory at six sharp. I ask the hostess if she's seen a blonde girl my age.

"Snow? Sure, I know her. She came in a half hour ago and ordered a mushroom calzone. Some creep barged in and began bugging her. The manager wanted to toss him but Snow said it was OK and left with him."

"Did this creep have a big beak?"

The hostess grins. "Sure did. And smelled baaad."

"Thanks. I'll take two pepperoni to go."

Now what? There's no shuttle to the Cone ranch and it'll take me hours to hoof it there. But I don't have a choice except to walk there. I promised I'd come.

24
Night Walk

My dive watch says 9:00 p.m. and, believe it or not, I'm still hoofing. In the dark it's hard to know I'm on the right road but I shake out the pebbles in my sneakers and brush off the bug the size of a walnut that skittered up my calf. A beetle? Nobody got killed by a beetle, did they? I'm OK with jellyfish and sand sharks but I'm not a bug guy. Like, yeech!

Minutes later, I reach the Cone house. Yaaaay! An instinct warns me not to go straight to the front door so I creep around the side and spy through one of the windows.

Prof Cone-Head is on the couch next to Fumi and the ugly one is poking his finger in the prof's nose like it's a sticky elevator button that refuses to light up. The prof just pulls his knees up to his chest. What a wuss! My dad may be a chair-sitter but he'd never let a slimeball like this push him around.

"Iz too late to back out - Con-ee!"

" - you promised to publish my book, *Butch's Revenge*. It's my crowning achievement!"

" - fool! Why would we help *you?*"

Hmm. I'm wondering the same thing.

 "Sheriff Shackle said you dug - "

" - shut up. When you needed money we gave it
you. You zink we do zis for favor? You are dummy!"

"You promised to help secure Butch's place in
history - "

" - foolish man - "

" - you'll destroy my career - "

" - zur career is stupid. Ve vant Cedar Leigh. Quit
stalling!"

Fumi jumps in. "We find out from computer that
Cedar Leigh is horse. Even ze stupid boy Deep Leetle
knows zis."

Stupid boy? Me?

Cone blurts, "I had to hold something back - "

" - zu don't trust us? Maybe you're not so dumb as
zu look."

Fumi pulls out a thin blue cigarette and lights up.
He exhales and shoots smoke out of his beak like a coal-
burning train engine.

"If I knew where Cedar Leigh is, I'd dig him up myself."

"Don't play dumb, profezzur. Ve digs holes here, there, everywhere. I hate cedar trees and zis miserable place. "

Romo kicks the sofa.

"People are coming to help me," bleats Cone.

Yeah, people ... *me*!

"For the last time, Butch-Cassidy-Bigshot, ver's Cedar Leigh?"

Romo smiles evilly in my direction. Has he seen me? No, he's just admiring his reflection in the window. Then Cone asks what I've been wondering all along.

"What have you done with Snow?"

25
A Very Short Fight

It's a close call, but between the two of them, Romo's uglier. Actually, he's the ugliest guy I've ever seen. He's six-five, 130 pounds, and has a long, lumpy beak that'd make a good snowboard course. Fumi is the nose-breaker of the two, even if he has to stand on a chair to do it. I figure he's more dangerous so I take him on first. I grab a loose board - praying it's not covered with spiders - and suck in a deep breath. Then I swing like a cleanup hitter in the World Series. What follows is the coolest explosion ever as the window shatters and wood and glass fly everywhere.

I lunge through the window and charge Fumi. The human bowling ball is ready for me.

"Leetle Deep! Come to me!"

We collide head-on and he levels me. So much for the taking-Fumi-out-first strategy.

I scramble up. "Get a move on, prof!"

I tug on the his arms but he's so stiff I can't pry him off the sofa. Part of the problem may be that Romo has a gun. It's not your basic plastic video game pistol, it's a shiny black magnet that sucks all emotion out of me except fear.

"Don't move, Conee. Fumi, tie up Professor Stupid while Deep and I go to truck." Romo wiggles his gun and points to the door. "Go to truck, Mr. Deep."

I "go to truck." Someone's there. Snow!

I climb in beside her and feel a sharp crack on the back of my skull. When I wake up, my head's pounding out a rhythm like an old Bluetorch video. Snow and I are bouncing up and down, hog-tied with plastic cord. I struggle to get loose and mutter, "How you doing?"

Sounds stupid. But what would *you* say?

"Relax," she says. "Tugging just makes it tighter - "

" - thanks. Wouldja believe it's my first time being tied up?"

We roll around in the pickup bed like loose watermelons. Overhead a billion stars swim in a white strip across the sky. I've seen the Milky Way for the first time. Hope it's not the last.

"How'd this happen?" Snow sobs.

"Could be worse," I say. "We could be doing homework."

OK. Stupid. I'm that scared.

"I shouldn't have asked you to come."

"Forget that and dream up a way to get us out of this. While you're at it, fill me in how your dad got mixed up with these bozos?"

"It's like this. Romo hired dad to authenticate Western stuff." Bump-bump. "Letters, photos, like that. In return, Romo promised to publish dad's book and gave him a cash advance." Bump-bump. "It's the book dad's been working on for years. It sounded too good to be true." She sucks up a sob. "And it was. Romo's stuff was phony and dad wouldn't OK it."

She takes a breath.

"Believe me, dad takes his history seriously. He wouldn't pass off fakes. Romo wanted the money back but dad had already spent it. That made Romo so angry he threatened to pin the fakes on *dad*. Dad was afraid people would believe Romo so he tried to buy him off by showing him Butch's letter. That boomeranged too!

"Honest, dad's not a bad guy."

"So the letter and jewelry are real?"

"Yup. But Romo thinks dad's holding out about where's Cedar Leigh."

"Well, is he? Does he know where Cedar Leigh is, I mean."

"No! He'd tell the Super if he knew ... you don't suppose Romo will hurt dad, do you?"

"Stop with your dad and worry about *us*." I'd wrap my arms around her if I could. I'd settle for feeling my arms, period.

"Romo said they're taking us to Grafton."

"Grafton, the ghost town? COWBOYLOVER said it's where Cedar Leigh is."

"COWBOYLOVER?"

"It's a long story."

"Yeah, Grafton is an abandoned Mormon settlement with only a meeting-house and cemetery left."

The truck brakes squeal as we fishtail to a stop in a cloud of dust. Fumi lowers the gate and I smell him before I see him.

"Leetle Deep and Leetle Snow. Zu are here! Za ghosts are vaiting! Ooooeee!"

Romo grabs me and Fumi grabs Snow and they drag us out of the truck and shove us through a gap in a barbed wire fence and into a tiny cemetery. How tiny? Hmm ... well, let's say smaller than a movie star's bathroom. Around us the grave markers of long-dead Utah settlers glow and float in the moonlight.

"Deep Leetle ... meet ze dead!" cackles Fumi. He loops a cord around a grave marker and re-ties me. "*Ciao*," he chirps. "Enjoy zur visit. Too bad no one comes here. Vat say zu, Romo? Two days with no water and Deep-Snow are toast?"

Romo spits on the nearest grave. "Tomorrow ze birds will eat zer big blue eyes for breakfast."

They're trying to scare us. And it's working.

"It could be days before anyone finds us," I whisper.

Fumi slams shut the gate and cackles again. "*Ciao*, leetle pest. Now ve find Cedar Leigh."

"You don't know where," yelps Snow. "You need us - "

" - ve don't need zu. Ze professor weel talk," snarls
Fumi. "Ve'll squeeze ze troof out of him like ze stupid
American ketchup." He demonstrates by twisting his fists.

Yikes! Tied up in the boonies, Snow and I might
shrivel up in the desert sun before anyone finds us.
Frantically, I crane my neck to read the inscriptions on the
headstones on my left.

Robert M. Berry, Killed by Indians, April 2, 1868.
Joseph S. Berry, Killed by Indians, April 2, 1868.

The Berry's can't save me now. I imagine my own
grave marker:

Dip Little, Killed By His Own Stupidity.

I turn to the right. Huh? Am I seeing things? In
shock, I stare at an inscription lit up by pale blue
moonlight.

R.I.P. My beloved Cedar Leigh.

26
The Big Dig

I scream even louder than the time my mom invited Fern Randall to my tenth birthday party by mistake.

"I found Cedar Leigh!"

Romo freezes.

"Deep is liar," he roars. "Beeg Deep Liar."

But I've hooked him like a trout. He and Fumi whisper in their mystery tongue and stalk back and forth. Romo shoves Fumi and Fumi windmills to stay upright.

Snows hisses, "For real?"

"Yeah, Cedar Leigh's *here*."

Romo closes in. His rank tobacco smell reminds me of the garbage under the pier after a storm.

"Vat you say, Leetle Deep?" He pokes me. "Say again."

"Cedar Leigh is under our feet."

Romo stares at the grave marker, transfixed. "Fumi! Get shovel from truck and dig, stupid, dig."

Fumi tries but after baking in the hot Utah sun for a hundred years the hard-packed earth crust is like concrete.

The shovel rebounds out of his hands and whacks him in the shoulder. Angered, he tosses it at me like a missile.

"You dig, scooterboy!"

"That's skaterboy, not scooterboy. Get it right!"

Romo mutters that Fumi is an idiot and slits the cord around my wrists. He snarls and exposes yellow gums and rotted teeth. If Butch were here he'd shoot Romo just to avoid having to look in his mouth.

I chip away slowly to buy time. It pays off when a sound cuts through the darkness like a switchblade. A car is coming our way.

But who's driving?

The sound distracts Fumi long enough that I'm able to nail him with the shovel. He sags like a bag of dirty laundry, giving me time to snip Snow's plastic cuffs. We hit the ground running as behind us Romo waves his pistol in frustration.

"Prepare for ze Wild West shutout!"

"That's *shootout*, you moron!"

Romo fires a shot. Nowhere close. "I keel ze one who takes *my* jewelry!"

Fumi is out cold.

The mystery car roars into the cemetery full speed. Big Dip is at the wheel. He clips Romo with the Bug's front fender and sends Romo flying like a beach ball at a Dodger game. I kick away his pistol and when Romo gets to his feet I send him flying again. This time he stays down for good. The whole thing is so cool I can't believe it's real.

Big Dip rushes over to Snow. "Don't believe we've been introduced."

That's how the shoot-out ends, with me wrapping my arms around Big Dip and Snow wrapping her arms around both of us. We stay that way until a second car skids to a stop beside us. My dad, Super Sandy and Prof Cone pile out. They stumble over like a trio of drunks on a bender.

"You're too late, older dudes. It's all over."

27
The Big Dig Continues

Within minutes a fleet of cars from the Park Service and sheriff's department has formed a circle around us, their headlights lighting up the scene like a movie set. Once dad's sure Big Dip and I are OK, he does a lap around the cemetery to calm down. Then he calls M to tell her Big Dip and I are in one piece.

Well, make that two pieces.

After that, dad, the Super and the sheriff huddle together pretending they're the ones in the know. Fat chance. They're so used to being the go-to adults with the answers that they muddle around asking each other the questions they should be asking *us*.

Prof Cone hugs Snow and says he's sorry but it's not his fault. Nobody listens. After a while, the sheriff debriefs me and Snow. We're the only ones who know the whole story.

"You mean the Cosezu brothers kidnapped you? But why?"

"Snow and I were on to them," I explain for the third time. Geez, this guy is slow. "They wanted us out of the way while they ran off with the jewelry before anyone got wise."

"Yeah," adds Snow. "Nobody figured out what they were up to. They could push my dad around but they couldn't push Dip around. They spooked and stashed us here."

I break in. "By accident they tied us up next to Cedar Leigh. Dumb luck. Ours, I guess. The jewelry from Butch's last robbery is ... *here*."

I stomp dramatically on the grave.

"Hmmm. Does this make sense to anyone?" the sheriff asks dad and Big Dip. He ignores the prof.

"The loot's here. Read the poem on Cedar Leigh's headstone if you don't believe me."

Shed not for her the bitter tear
Nor give the heart to vain regret
'Tis but the casket that lies here
The gem that filled it sparkles yet.

"That's code for, The Jewelry Is Buried Here."

"I'm not convinced," says my dad.

"Listen. It's like this. The knuckleheads " - all eyes watch a deputy stuff the handcuffed Romo and Fumi in a squad car - "dug under *cedar trees* instead of *Cedar Leigh*."

"I'll be darned." Super Sandy kicks the mound.

Big Dip makes faces at Romo and Fumi through the squad car window. Then he rests his hands on dad's shoulder. "Trust Dip on this, son."

"Hmm," says my dad. "Hmm."

"Don't you trust me, dad?"

"Uh, yeah," he says, but it comes out sort of forced.

"OK, get the shovel," says Sheriff Shackle. That cinches it. With the law on board, my dad comes around too.

Professor Cone pipes up. "I'm convinced that Dip has read Butch's mind." He hesitates. "Better even than me.

"I applaud you, Dip Little." He holds up two fingers in a salute. "When I began my own Butch Cassidy studies years ago no one took me seriously, either. Those were challenging times for me personally - "

Big Dip cuffs the prof on the shoulder. "Give it a rest where we can't hear you. Heh, heh."

I take a deep breath and dig. Six swings and I break through the sun-baked crust to a rotted casket.

Thunk!

I feel a moment of doubt. What if this is a sucker play and there's no loot? What if there's a note saying: "Gotcha, dummy, see ya 'round!" With flashlights pointing from all directions, lighting up my stupidity or success for all to see, I pry open the rotted lid.

Inside is a plain wood box.

The prof can't control himself any longer. He lunges forward and the sheriff has to grab him by the collar and yank him back. "Hold your horses, Cone. This ain't yours, it's the people's." He turns to me. "Do the honors."

Dad nods and Big Dip gives me a thumbs-up. I wedge a screwdriver under the box's rusty catch and jerk it back and forth until the lock snaps. Snow slips her finger in and lifts the lid.

Flashlight beams bounce off a tangled heap of gold and jewelry that's waited in the dark for a hundred years!

28
Last Ramble

It's late morning before we get back to the lodge. Not that it matters, I'm too wired to sleep. At noon we go to town for a celebratory lunch. A crowd is waiting at the restaurant, the word has gotten out about the mystery.

A *People* magazine reporter sticks her nose in my face and demands that I pose for her photographer. "Smile, handsome!" She bares her teeth like a mountain lion about to tear off a jackrabbit's head.

Dad rescues me and steers me into the Bit 'n Spur Grill. Super Sandy and the Cones are at the table of honor with Big Dip. A waitress sets cake in front of us and I gobble mine in two bites, then eat dad's and grandpa's too. Rain would want me to.

The *People* reporter turns to bugging the grill manager. "I'm not leaving until I get a picture of Dip Little kissing the blonde. Get me the shot and there's something in it for you."

A CNN stringer pushes in. "Wild West outlaws. Jewels. Teenagers named Dip, Rain and Snow. This story has it all."

The reporter and the stringer argue over who gets first interview with me, until the manager douses them both with a pitcher of water and points to the door. Even then the journalist types head my way with mikes and cameras. Click, click, click.

My BlackBerry vibrates in my pocket.

R U HOME? G.

G? Is that who's been texting me? The only G I know is ... no, can't be, not that gremmie from the beach, Grody Albright. Where's he get the nerve to text *me?*

Super Sandy lifts his beer. "I propose a toast to Dip Little." He sucks down his beer in one swallow and orders another.

Dad lifts his glass. "To my son. I'm proud of you."

I raise my Coke. "To Big Dip, the greatest man I know. And to Snow, the greatest girl."

Beer mugs and wine glasses wave in the air with toasts.

Maybe I forgot to mention that there's a gold ring with a blood red ruby on the table in front of us. Sheriff Shackle has locked away Butch's jewelry for safekeeping except for this one ring. Even the sheriff, with the approval of the governor, thinks a certain someone deserves it as a reward for solving the Butch Cassidy mystery.

The only problem is, no one agrees who's the certain someone. The sheriff says it's me cuz I dug up Cedar Leigh. I say that if not for Snow I wouldn't have heard of Cedar Leigh. Snow says that if not for Big Dip she'd still be hog-tied in Grafton.

"So let's toast Big Dip," suggests Super Sandy. Everyone raises a mug and cheers.

"Speech!" cries Snow.

Big Dip waves his hand as if to say, forget-about-it. But the crowd bangs its silverware on the tables and chants, "Speech, speech, speech!" He gives in and holds the ruby ring aloft while motioning for quiet.

"This ring is wasted on an old man." He smiles from ear to ear ... he's digging it, so to speak. "It should go to a girl just as beautiful." He takes Snow's hand and slips it on her finger.

He's not done.

"My memory may slip now and then ... but there's one person I'll *never* forget." He raises his glass. "To my grandson, whose mystery is only beginning!"

The crowd stomps and hoots, even if I'm nonplussed. What's he mean, my mystery's beginning? The Butch Cassidy mystery is officially over and done with.

"Let's not forget the secret hero in all this."

"Who's that?" demand a dozen voices.

"Why, Cedar Leigh!"

The restaurant throng roars in agreement. People shout and gesture and toast their boyfriends and girlfriends, pets and favorite bands. Strangers offer to buy me margaritas. The media, locked out, poke their cameras in through the windows.

My dad leans over to whisper, "When this hits home you'll be a celebrity in Santa Monica."

Me? The funny thing is, since we found the jewelry I haven't spent two seconds wondering how it'll play at home. Me, a hero? I was just having fun. As for The Peach, I don't care anymore.

Snow whispers, "Where's your grandpa gone?"

Good question. Somehow Big Dip has slipped off without me noticing. Just like that, I snap back to my job at home. Rescuing Big Dip is *my* job, after all. I look but he's not in the men's room or talking to the media. A busboy carrying out the trash points me to the back door and a dusty trail that leads away from the restaurant.

I feel a stab of worry. Hope he's not scared. Does he realize I'll come for him? Guiltily, I remember a time when the poppies teased me so bad I got pissed having to track him down. How could I have been so selfish? I'm the luckiest kid in the whole world.

"I'm coming, Big Dip."

Up ahead I spot a fallen-down slab of Navajo sandstone. A halo of white hair pokes over the top. I figure it's Big Dip, resting and checking out the view over Crater Hill.

"A-ha, I found you!"

No response.

"Grandpa?"

I climb over the sandstone slab and drop down next to Big Dip. I rest my hand on his forehead, like mom does when he comes home from a long ramble. His brow is cool and his eyes are closed but it seems to me he's smiling.

"Grandpa?"

29
A Gift

When a Little dies - no matter where, no matter when - they get planted in the family plot in Concord, Massachusetts. Every Little for generations has been buried there.

The funeral service begins with the usual hymn and the usual prayer, the one about, *Knock and the door will be opened.* The minister says the usual stuff that tips you off he never met the dearly departed. You can bet he'll work in something about the Little's landing in America four hundred years ago, though.

Talk about your Ancient History.

When dad and I get home from Zion, the planning for Big Dip's funeral is in high gear. The Concord church is reserved and mom has made plane reservations to Boston. Four identical suitcases line up beside the front door.

It's either pipe up now or my promise to Big Dip will get buried six feet under along with him.

"Uh, M&D - "

- mom's eyes are red from crying and dad is shell-shocked. What I'm gonna say will go over like a lead balloon.

"Honey, this is hard for all of us. You and Big Dip are so close." Mom blows her nose. "*Were* so close."

"I gotta tell you - "

" - what's wrong, honey?" Mom strokes my forehead like she used to do with Big Dip.

" - grandpa didn't want to be buried back East."

"What?" exclaims dad.

Mom shakes her head and cuts in. "Of course he did."

"No - he wanted to be" - I point to the blue-green Pacific - "out there."

"In the ... *ocean*?"

M&D do the head-shaking thing as a duet. You'd think I wanted to dump Big Dip's ashes off the Ferris wheel on the pier.

Jesse walks in. "That's cool," she says. "Grandpa was so cool." Her BlackBerry beeps. It's probably Chopper trying to get her back from Sid who got her back from Chopper.

"No way," says dad firmly. "Something that important he'd tell your mom and me."

"Honey, maybe you misunderstood."

"No! He trusted *me*."

Mom cocks her head and dad paws with his foot like he'd rather be somewhere else. They're thinking that I get in fights and waste time at the beach. I don't even do my homework without being reminded.

I'm tempted to grab my surfboard and run down Bicknell Hill to the beach. It'd be easy to let them do what they want. Why should I put up with them assuring each other that there's no way Big Dip trusted ... *me*.

But I promised.

Dad hooks up his sister in Concord and puts her on the speaker. "Marj ... new development ... Dip has some info."

"Uh, Aunt Marjorie, Dip here. It's like this. Grandpa wanted his ashes laid in the ocean."

A short silence, then pandemonium.

"I don't believe it. Uh-uh! Why'd he tell *you*? A ... a ... *skater*! You're no better than an ... an ... *outlaw* - "

- dad's face explodes at the word *outlaw*. Everyone starts yelling, even Aunt Marjorie's third husband, Winston. He reminds M&D that he's a lawyer too and he'll fight this in court if necessary.

"Don't make stupid threats," warns my dad. "And apologize to my son while you're at it."

Go dad!

Mom yells, "You don't know the first thing about Dip."

It's the new M&D! But enough with adults freaking out.

"It's not about *me*, it's about *grandpa*," I say. That gets their attention. Adults just need a firm hand now and then.

"I can't tell you why he trusted me but he did."

"What'd he say exactly?" asks Aunt Marjorie more calmly.

"He said his trust was a gift."

"Huh?" says Jesse. "Trust *you*? He was old, not stupid."

"Enough, Jesse," snaps my dad.

"He said dad would understand."

Mom turns to dad. "Well, Rob, do you?"

My dad speaks so softly I can barely hear. "When I was fourteen and Marjorie was thirteen, a family in New Haven got burned out of their house. They had nowhere to go."

Marjorie jumps in. "Big Dip gave us each a thousand bucks and told us not to say how we spent it. His gift was his - "

" - *trust*," finishes my dad.

Winston still doesn't get it. "That's a lot of so-what. In *my* legal opinion - "

" - oh, shut up, Winston," snaps my aunt. "It's OK, Dip. You do what Big Dip wanted. And I'm sorry I called you an *outlaw*."

Well, I *am* an outlaw. But whatever. I won't argue.

30
Cool As Peppermint

It's cool as peppermint on Santa Monica Bay three mornings later when dad and I set off from the pier in a rented motor dinghy. We leave early so we can finish our business before the swell picks up. At first I didn't understand why mom and Jesse aren't coming. But last night M&D talked 'til late and this morning mom hugged me and said, "Just you and dad go."

Did I mention that maybe I'm too hard on mom?

Dad holds the plain wood box with Big Dip's ashes in his lap. Hard to believe there's anything there. Eighty years of a man's life? Whoa. We hit the chop and the box jumps, but it's OK. I figure Big Dip enjoys the ride.

The sky is foggy and overcast. Typical Santa Monica. In a few hours the marine layer will burn off and the sky will turn blue. Every Local knows that. But now the sky and ocean are like two blankets, one gray and the other green. Me, dad and Big Dip are salami-ed in between.

I steer to the spot Big Dip chose and cut the engine. The only sound is the waves slapping at the dinghy sides. Dad hands me the box but I shove it back like in a game of hot potato.

"You do it, dad."

"No, he said you."

OK, grandpa. I'll do it. Although when we sailed I didn't believe inside that you'd die. Back then I didn't believe anyone I loved would die.

So how do I lay you to rest? Dump your ashes in a blob? Shake them like parmesan cheese on a plate of spaghetti? When I think of eating spaghetti with Big Dip, the tears bust out and spill down my cheeks. I want to shout, "I can't do it!" so loud they'll hear me all the way to John Adams Middle School.

The feeling passes and I slip the lid off the box. Before I can dream up a prayer a gust of wind snatches Big Dip's ashes. They swirl in a small tornado above me and are gone.

Dad and I sit in silence. Time passes. Maybe it's a long time or maybe it isn't.

"Ready?" Dad reaches for the cord to fire up the motor.

"You go without me. I'll swim in from here."

Before dad can argue, I kick off my flip-flops and strip off my t-shirt. I dive overboard, surface, and pick out lifeguard tower 25. A swell lifts me up and I glimpse the *Nuevos* working up a trick on Bicknell Hill. Rain is waiting for me on the seawall and Grody is lurking by the lifeguard tower.

Later on, Rain will fill me in on what went down while I was setting Big Dip free. The *Nuevos* were checking out Duane's new Alpha Team skateboard when who should stroll along arm in arm but Kyle Gibson and The Peach.

"Where's the Flakeboard King?" demanded Kyle, still wearing his knee brace. "In the loony bin with his grandpa?"

The *Nuevos* ignored him but Kyle's not gonna be blown off in front of The Peach. He does his monkey dance and chants, "Check it out. I could be the Flakeboard King *or* his grandpa. They're *both* nuts!"

Then Duane - of all the guys, Duane! - stomps on Kyle's foot and dumps him on his butt. Kyle jumps up and charges Duane like the dying bull in a bullfight.

Not a smart move.

Duane pivots like he's doing a three-sixty on his board and Trace steps up and slaps Kyle hard across the face. Even Grody gets in the act by taunting Kyle from the lifeguard tower. Later on Grody cops to texting me too. But that's for another time.

Just like that a huge welt springs up on Kyle's nose. Suddenly the famous tough-guy is only a clown. He snarls at the *Nuevos* and sprints off, leaving The Peach behind.

Later on, Rain tells me that. But when I first come ashore, neither of us says a word. A few *Viejos* are checking out the break but they must think the sets are too shrimpy cuz they keep on yakking. I try to pinpoint where I laid Big Dip's ashes. North of tower 25? Or south? It's only been a couple minutes and I can't be sure.

How could I forget? I know this stretch of beach like my backyard. When I was small I crawled on the waterline and collected shells. I built sand castles and forts.

Every summer I learned something new. Swimming. Boogey-boarding. Surfing.

I picked out the *Nuevos* to be my friends and together we ruled Bicknell Hill, imitating the mysterious cool of the *Viejos*. Nothing, and I mean nothing, blows the cool of a *Viejo*. *Viejos* - some are older than my dad! - never hurry. They show up at Bay Street if and when they feel like it, and surf only if the sets are worth it. If it's blown-out they clump together on the seawall and talk stuff we *Nuevos* don't have a clue about.

From the first day my mom walked me across the street to the beach and I saw those guys in their sleek black wetsuits, I wanted to be one of them. Nothing in the whole world is as cool as a *Viejo* on a summer evening. They perch on the tailgates of their pickups, lined up overlooking the ocean like sea birds facing the setting sun. Or hunch on the seawall, never changing expression, swapping stories of Bay Street back in the day.

I wanted to be a *Viejo* on my special beach so bad I could taste it. But all of a sudden it's not my beach. It's just a sheet of gray sky stacked on a sheet of green water and I can't remember where I laid my grandpa's ashes.

Rain reads my mind. "Where'd you dump 'em? Did they float?"

I point at the ocean in a vague sort of way. Big Dip's ashes are sailing out there, somewhere in the deep water of the Pacific beyond the buoys that mark the no-swim zone. Isn't that all anyone needs to know?

Some day I'll explain what it was like to set Big Dip free. Some day I'll sort out the confusion inside me: the holding-onto and the letting-go. Some day I'll give you the lowdown on how it feels to be a fourteen year-old boy.

Just not quite yet.